CARRY

ME

ACROSS

THE

WATER

Random House New York

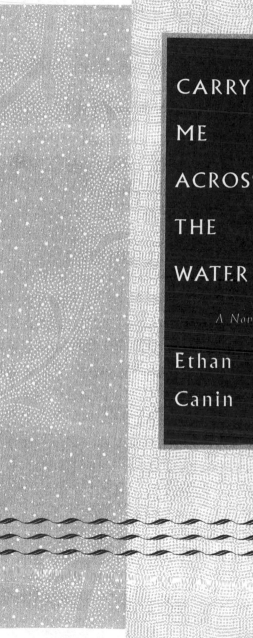

CARRY

ME

ACROSS

THE

WATER

A Novel

Ethan
Canin

Library of Congress Cataloging-in-Publication Data
Canin, Ethan.
Carry me across the water / Ethan Canin—1st ed.
p.   cm.
ISBN 0-679-45679-1 (alk. paper)
1. Jewish men—Fiction.   2. Beer industry—Fiction.
3. Pittsburgh (Pa.)—Fiction.   4. World War, 1939-1945—Fiction.
5. Immigrants—Fiction.   I. Title.
PS3553.A495 C37   2001   813'.54—dc21   00-051812

Printed in the United States of America on acid-free paper
Random House website address: www.atrandom.com
9 8 7 6 5 4 3 2
First Edition

Book design by J. K. Lambert

For Barbara, Amiela, and Ayla

ACKNOWLEDGMENTS

I am grateful to many for help with this book. For aid in research, I am indebted to the University of Iowa Arts & Humanities Initiative. For various favors, minor and major, I thank Wally Plahutnik, Nate Brady, Jane Martin, Frankie Jones, Chuck Sellers, Frank Conroy, Michael Goldman, Jen Wagner, Hans Wendl, Connie Brothers, Paul Buttenwieser, Steve Sellers, Wendy Deutelbaum, Neil MacFarquhar, Scott Lasser, E. L. Doctorow, and Michele Bronson. For great gifts of time and effort, I am deeply grateful to Alex Gansa, Dayna Goldfine, John McGhee, Evan Stone, Leslie Maksik, Chard deNiord, Dan Geller, Sue Schuler, Chuck Thompson, Virginia Canin, Michael Chabon, Jon Maksik, Mark Leary, Kate Medina, Stuart Canin, Maxine Groffsky, Veronica Windholz, Po Bronson, and Barbara Canin—words cannot thank you enough.

CARRY

ME

ACROSS

THE

WATER

———————————————————————

My Most Divine Umi—

You cannot imagine how I long for you.

When I think of my real life (or shall I say my past life? For this, now, is my real life) so much of it vanishes—Sounzan, the mountain, even my beloved parents—and all that remains of my time on earth are the days that I have spent with you. And two of these days you know nothing about! Are you aware that I spent the Saturday before my departure with you? No, how could you know?

You and Kakuzo, with little Teiji in his basket, walked that morning to the inlet of turtles, and Kakuzo carried a gift melon, no doubt offered in honor of Teiji's birth. You shared it, then brought Teiji to the water and dipped his tiny feet. I believe I saw in Kakuzo, as he stood at the edge of the shore stones, a hesitancy to touch the baby: is it possible? I know such details, my love, because I was in the cherry trees watching you.

My life I give to the two of you.

From my hiding place, I watched Teiji closely. He is quite still—a sign in a baby, I believe, of the artist's vision. I believe he is watching everything: the folds of cotton at the rim of his basket, the pale Sounzan sky, the mountain painting itself on the quiet of Lake Ashi. He is watching and recording, and one day he will astonish you. Perhaps he will draw a grove of cherries and, in it, hidden by leaves and branches, a heart that is plundered, watching you. Or perhaps he will attempt to draw the mountain itself, inverted in the lake, perfection as it exists and therefore the stumblestone of all who would attempt its capture. Allow me, if I might, to hope.

And then there was Tuesday morning, the morning I reported to my regiment, when on the way to the Odawara train I passed by Kakuzo's shop. I do not know what I was planning to do. Our beautiful Sounzan was still in darkness, and I had thoughts of entering the shop and telling Kakuzo the truth; but when I came to the window, there he was inside, sewing a mat, and before I had the chance to enter, I saw that you were there also, next to him, on the floor on a tatami watching the baby, and I believe that what I saw in your face was sorrow.

I will believe that what you were thinking about, Umi, was what had occurred between us.

This is my conviction. Perhaps I am mistaken, and in that case the fate that surely awaits me here is the better of the two that are possible. Yet as I rode the train that morning away from Sounzan, I could not help but believe that your melancholy was because you too desired the miracle for which I myself had once hoped, the miracle for which now, as I face the prospect of never seeing you again, I cannot help but hope once again.

Here on Aguni, I have constructed a passable rendition of the world. The island, and my life where I have hidden myself, I will describe to you in an-

other letter. Perhaps it is different from how you imagine: after dark, I venture into the open for food and water, wary at every step. The soldiers are still about, even at night, but at least the snakes, which can drop upon a man from the tree limbs, are in their torpor then. And I am able, miraculously, and thanks to the efforts of carrying such items at great pains into the jungle, to read the poems of Basho and to study the prints of Gaho and Hogai, as well as to continue my own development in oils, a few of which I have carried here with me as well (thinned with kerosene, which is in adequate supply). This indeed is wondrous for me: not just to be able to work—and there are no distractions at all, here, my divine Umi—but to spend my days with these three great teachers of our heritage. Perhaps I will one day be able to tell you what I have learned of the eye and the romance it carries on, quietly and in a most halting manner, with the veiled beauty of the world.

And if they find me here—forgive me, but I know the efforts of our emperor have begun to sour—if they find me here, I plan to show them the Hogai. For this, I must hope that it is a man of sympathy who is the first to enter. For how can the beauty of those paintings not bring peace to such a heart, as it has to mine?

Umi, I know that it is likely you will never see this letter, yet I write in the hope that you yourself might have written a similar one, perhaps, to me; though I am aware, as well, that I most probably will never see that one either.

Yet I remain,

in most exquisite devotion—

There is no signature. August Kleinman has a copy of this letter in his condominium in Boston, framed in box-jointed mahogany and calligraphed in a very fine, small hand, one of the few items he brought with him from the house in Newton when he moved. Next to it are two good-sized Francis Bacons and a dark Morandi, and, on the mantel, a porcelain cup containing several dull gold teeth and an alabaster brooch. Above the cup hangs another mahogany frame, from which the original letter, in Japanese, has been removed and in which only the pale rectangles of unfaded backing remain, rimmed by yellow, where for thirty years the rice paper had blocked the assaults of the sun.

⌇⌇⌇⌇⌇⌇⌇⌇⌇⌇⌇⌇⌇⌇⌇⌇⌇⌇⌇⌇

When August Kleinman was eighteen years old, a particularly florid eighteen—ruby-faced, wiry-armed, bursting with appetites that were so new to him as to seem the appetites of someone else entirely—he was invited to the Fordham University field house by his friend Mickey White, to watch the Fordham Rams practice football. Mickey White had made the varsity team. He and August had grown up together on Beach 28th Street near Seagirt Boulevard in Wavecrest, a Jewish alley of peeling bungalows a quarter-mile from the Atlantic Ocean on the Rockaway peninsula in Queens, and had been friends since the fifth grade, when August had arrived in New York. Mickey was at Fordham because his hair was red and his name might have been Irish, though he and August had attended not only the same high school but the same synagogue as well. Mickey was a year older than August and two years ahead of him in school. August was a junior at Far Rockaway High on the day he crossed the East River on the Long Island Rail Road, then caught the subway north to the Fordham campus in Rose Hill. In his hand he carried a square-folded copy of the *New York Post* and in his pocket a bootlegger's flask of diluted Scotch whiskey, which he had poured off from his stepfather's dusty cabinet. At Penn Station he had added a little water for caution. He wasn't even sure he would drink it, yet he wanted something in case his courage failed him. For some time now, courage had occupied his thoughts.

As he sat in the flickering sway of the tunnel shadows, he studied the scores in the *Post*. That Mickey White had made the Fordham squad was news all over Wavecrest, and though August was only intermittently interested in sports, he was obliged to pay close attention to the team. Mickey White, as it turned out, mattered very little in the success or failure of the Rams. He was a second-string blocking back and a third-string end—he rarely even made it into a game—but in the collection of bungalows between Sea-girt Boulevard and the Atlantic Ocean, he remained a figure of veneration among the children, as well as one of curiosity among their immigrant parents; August, as Mickey's friend, took it upon himself to become the neighborhood expert in his endeavors. Fordham in those days was a national powerhouse. Their games were on the radio every week, and they had been nearly unbeat-able while Mickey and August were in elementary school. The Seven Blocks of Granite had graduated now, but Fordham was still felt to have a good shot at the Sugar Bowl. In the first game of the new season they had beaten Holy Cross by three touchdowns and a field goal, and in the fourth quarter of that game August had heard Mickey White's name announced over the radio, substituting in the backfield once the lead had become insurmountable. This was 1940.

August himself had never played tackle football, and as he walked down the ramp in Rose Hill that autumn morning between brick stanchions to the Fordham field, demarked by a crumbling cork track, the sounds of thudding bodies frightened him. He could hear the wallop of leather and a chorus of stamps and thuds as though not men but horses were engaged below him on the green. He paused to compose himself. Then he came around the corner onto the track, where across the grass the team, in fabulous red-and-white jerseys, was running through drills of open-field tackling. Two lines faced each other across fifteen yards of trampled turf, and one at a time the end player would loose himself, fake and cut toward the opposing squad, and be brought down by a man on defense.

How August, a refugee from Europe and a stranger to the game, came to participate in that drill was a matter that would ring in his memory even after he had grown old. He stood watching the team, at first frightened by the violence, then drawn to it. He was not a timid boy, yet his boldness, such as it was, had always been in the service of self-preservation. This is what his short life had taught him. Now, when he noticed the door to the locker room standing open, he walked in. How could he have done so? A sense of the tempting world stood just beyond him, had stood there for some time now, a glinting panorama of possibility that clutched him whenever the train turned on 54th Avenue and hurtled, clacking and swaying, toward the East River. And always, to counter it, was the sense of his mother as well, his mother in her patched-up sweaters, his mother with all her warnings, rinsing the kosher plates at the sink. Inside the locker room now, he stood behind the immense metal door—a door that seemed big enough for cattle to pass through—preparing a look of bafflement in case onc was needed. But nobody approached him. He pinched a drink from the flask and, though at first its fiery taste only alarmed him further, within a moment he felt vigor inflate his chest and then spread to his limbs. Behind the first stand of lockers he found an unattended bus-bin of numbered Fordham jerseys, and another of canvas knee shorts, and hanging from a pole alongside the showers a selection of the jointed shoulder pads, thick canvas thighguards, and leather headgear that the players wore in practice.

On the field, a break came in the drill. August—in a uniform now—slipped out the door onto the grass and found himself at the end of the line on defense. When he reached the front, the player from the line opposite began high-stepping upfield toward him, feinting with his shoulders, and August took three running steps forward, planted his feet, and launched himself.

After he was discovered and ejected, he was escorted back to the locker room by one of the Fordham coaches, Paul Wyzcozki, who sat on a swivel stool watching as August removed the uniform, donned his own plain gray pants and wrinkled white shirt, and walked to the exit. Coach Wyzcozki then stood by the other huge door as August opened it and stepped halfway out onto the street. Suddenly, the coach said, in a not unfriendly voice, "Where do you learn that?"

August turned. Paul Wyzcozki had played offensive tackle for the Brooklyn Dodgers in the National Football League, a giant of a man with a giant's effortless sonorations, though his head was of a refined appearance. He blinked his eyes and snapped one hand down upon the other. "Such a big tremendous blow."

"I don't know," August said. "I really don't know."

"Who is it you watch for?"

August didn't understand.

"Who are you watching for? You are Villanova, yes?"

August fled up the street then, ran block after block through the quiet streets of Rose Hill toward the subway, borne on by powerful feelings of shame but also, as he boarded the D train and rode it through its first screeching turn toward the water, by a mounting ecstasy; as the train picked up speed and swayed in longer, rattling arcs under the Harlem River into Manhattan, he repeated the coach's words, imitated the respectful smack of one hand upon the other. He was shaking. *You are Villanova, yes?* It was not until bed that night, lying awake as the apartment grew quiet, that he understood it was not the coach's words that had set him quivering but the tackle itself, some powerful surge of violence that was utterly new to him. *Such a big tremendous blow!* It was the first time he'd ever felt such release, the moment of impact and the moment thereafter, the sensation of lightness at contact, the complete departure of his earthbound being.

That year at Chanukah, Mickey White told the tale up and down Seagirt Avenue. August was more than a little pleased, not only for the ferocity of the tackle, which Mickey embellished with a swoop of his open hand like a striking torpedo, but also for the gumption of his own maneuver, with which he had surprised himself deeply. He was in the doorway between boyhood and manhood, and any piece of evidence that indicated his fearlessness came upon him like a sudden break in the mist that enveloped his trajectory. He caught a glimpse of himself as a man. Not the halting, indolent creature he was now but a person of action: unflinching, dauntless, a breaker of the rules that otherwise would not have afforded much to a ruby-faced, ill-proportioned boy like himself.

You are Villanova, yes?

The sensation of flight, the corporal ease of the contact, the physical law of colliding momentums carried to perfection: he was an old man now, but when he recalled his days, he could still feel the jolt of the tackle.

H e was, in fact, seventy-eight years old. Wealthy, a father of three, a widower—his life had shown him the fruit and dirt of the world: he had killed one man and possibly a second, told Lyndon Johnson he was a coward after paying two thousand dollars to meet him, grown rich in a business that was abidingly anti-Semitic, beaten all the odds, and then lost the great love of his life before returning, if not to his former self, then at least to a man who could pass as that. He was in decline but not yet down. He still rose at dawn, still walked briskly in the streets of the Back Bay as they were being cleaned by the mechanical sweepers, still tipped his fedora to cops and beer deliverymen, still poured a Glenfiddich every evening and listened with tears in his eyes to

Pablo Casals play the Bach Suites for Cello. The only thing that was different was that now he spent much of the daylight hours remembering. He was retired—that was nine tenths of it—but still, as he walked every morning in the glistening streets, he found himself involuntarily transported to the past. This incident that had occurred, it was far from the worst thing he had ever done. Yet he could not forget it.

Perhaps arrogance had been the cause—certainly he had always been arrogant. This he was aware of in a way that only further proved his arrogance; that is, he saw no reason to change, had never seen reason to. It was by the strength of his own initiative, after all, that he had risen to his position in the world—all alone, perhaps, but more than comfortable. And his successes had come against the advice of everyone he knew. If that was what arrogant was, then he was proud to be so. In 1946 his uncle Manny had urged him to go into the ice-block-delivery business—this was the kind of guidance he'd been given—and his stepfather, on his deathbed, had told him he should never have married a Gentile. Such were the forces that had almost toppled him. He considered arrogance a virtue.

When people lost their temper with him, "arrogant" is what they said. "You arrogant man," the United stewardess had whispered last week as they reached cruising altitude in the cloudless sky west of Tokyo. "You arrogant son of a bitch," his partner had called him fifty years ago when he discovered that Kleinman hadn't yet ordered a new copper fermenting vessel for the wort (though later, in a toast over the outcome, the two of them had raised a glass of lager to arrogance). He had been shocked to find the very word in the year-end efficiency report from his first boss, a bankrupt Maine blueberry farmer who ran the sales force, such as it was, at Portland Suitcase. "Good initiative," the man had written fifty-five years ago on his evaluation card. "Average intelligence. Clean dress. Arrogant." Kleinman had laughed—as accurate an appraisal as he'd ever been given. He still had the card in a shoe box. "I guess arrogance runs in the family," he had heard his son Jimmy say to his daughter-in-law last week as the bedroom door closed down the hall.

I n the spring of 1941, his junior year at Far Rockaway High School, he met the girl he would marry. Ginger Pella was her name, a Naples Italian from a rambling family of merchants living half a mile west on Edgemere Avenue, recently moved down from Boston. She still had an accent; he'd already lost his. She had the coloring of the Jewish girls in Wavecrest, though all the lines had been straightened: the hair, the nose, the cheeks. Yet there remained in the flatness of her face against the sharpness of her features a play of shadows that reminded August one afternoon of his mother. Ginger was next to him in chemistry section at Far Rockaway High, mixing bicarbonate of soda into an Erlenmeyer flask and recording her observations in a speckled black laboratory notebook. She was a good student; he was not. He was watching her technique with the chemicals, trying to discern what he was supposed to do with the three small bottles of powder in front of him, when she dropped her head slightly in annoyance and threw her hair back over her shoulder; at that moment something ticked in his desire. He set down his own flask and stared at her. He did not fully understand her resemblance to his mother, for it would have frightened him; yet he almost did, aware of it like a memory he could not quite summon: the delicate concave plain between lip and nose—so that the mouth appeared independent of the other features, a recumbent red animal on a bed—and the eyes, as if alone inside a frame. He turned to the scarred slate laboratory bench, and then the three stoppered vials of powder arrayed across it like hazardous mysteries, but he could not stop himself from sneaking glances back in her direction. The distinctness of her features, the way they were minutely too far from one another, reminded him of the vaguely Egyptian profiles set in stone atop Far Rockaway's colonnade, which, when he turned back to the window, impressed him suddenly as a great carved testament to his ignorance. He looked again at Ginger. He found, in fact, that he could not proceed without returning, every few moments, to her face. The appeal of her dark eyes was also maternal, he noticed in a vague manner—gentleness, and the quality, when she finally returned his gaze, that she was looking upon a rascal. This too was his mother. August as a boy was neither schooled in the architecture of human character nor interested in it, yet when he finally asked directions about the experiment they were performing, and then dutifully poured twenty-five milliliters of sodium bicarbonate into his empty decanter, he was nearly paralyzed by the powerful yearning he felt for her and at the same time by the hint in himself that she was, somehow, forbidden.

A year later, in the crucifix-hung back-side parlor of her parents' dingy walk-up along the train tracks, the two of them were
discovered by her older brother, Santo, returning early from
work. Ginger's plain yellow blouse was open to her waist. Santo
was a small man but ten years older than August; he removed his
coat, held it out to Ginger, and said, "Cover yourself up."

"Santo," Ginger said, without taking the coat from her
brother's hand, "this is August."

"Now it's Jew-boy charity?" said Santo, through his teeth. "I
said cover it up." He dropped the coat over Ginger's torso. Then
he carefully removed his wristwatch, followed by his hat. "Cover
it up! And move away from the stinking whitefish." He was wearing shiny loafers and his tie was neatly knotted. He set his hat and
watch on the table, loosened the tie with his right hand, then with
the knuckles of his left struck August hard across the face. August's eyes filled. He couldn't help it: he had never been punched
in his life. But in a moment he found himself in a boxer's stance
that he had seen only in photos in the *Post*. Santo kicked him in
the knee, and when August bent forward to steady his rubbery
leg, Santo wound up and booted him like a ramrod across the
chest. August's breath left him; he staggered backward onto the
couch, amazed at the swiftness and completeness of his defeat.
But in the pause it took the older man to kneel and reposition the
shiny loafer on his foot, August suddenly got his wind, along with
an exhilarating surge of strength, and stood up, launching a jack-
hammer right that sent Santo tumbling back against the door
frame. Then August closed his hands over his face and let himself
be beaten.

It took a month for the bruises to clear. But the punch he'd landed—that, even more than the beating, he could not forget: the surprising cooperation of physics, the effortless transfer of force. He'd felt Santo on the other end of his fist, but only fleetingly, some half-represented compression of his weight, like a fish at the end of a line. And at the same time he again felt the recognition of something hard at the center of his own character, something immovable in the disorderly half-plan that he was now understanding to be his life.

~~~~~~~~~~~~~~~~~~~~~~~~~~~~~

D riving out from La Guardia to his son's apartment in Brooklyn Heights this morning, there had been some unpleasantness in the cab: Kleinman had called the driver a cheat and been obliged to disembark, among furious car horns and in a drizzle, on an overpass of the Brooklyn-Queens Expressway. From there, he had walked half a mile on arthritic knees in the rain, pulling his bag on its wheels, until he stumbled on a rental agency. By some piece of luck they had a Lincoln on the lot, and since he owned one—it was worth the money not to be confused—he paid extra and took it. The new one had all kinds of gadgets that confused him, but by ignoring them he was able to drive. And again luck favored him: down the block from Jimmy and Claudine's brownstone he found a parking space. Backing into it took some time, but it was a legal spot and not far at all from Jimmy's front door. He didn't believe in omens; nonetheless, this was a good one.

In the events of the past years he took no solace other than the relief of what he knew to be his toughness in the world. Now and then, unpredictably, his mind returned to Santo Pella and that punch. And from there to Santo's death, twenty years later, when a garbage truck crossed the median and pinned him against the pilings at the mouth of the Sumner Tunnel in Boston—Kleinman of course suspected this had not been an accident. But he himself had lived quite a long time, and the deaths of others, even those long in the past, had begun to produce in him a dreadful elation— the feeling in a dream of being pursued, the terror and jubilation of escape. Even in daylight sometimes he would snap back, as though from a nightmare. From the last cruel fate of the world he had thus far escaped. And this was not because he was a conciliator. Parking the Lincoln, he again jerked awake from his morbid thoughts.

Claudine and Jimmy had invited him for Yom Kippur, and to baby-sit his new grandson, Asher, who by now would be nearly three months old. He tried to picture a three-month-old, but all that came to mind was Ginger in a white nightgown—tears came to his eyes—quieting him in the hall after she'd put Jimmy to bed. He shuddered—1949? There was no reason to be afraid. He'd been there, after all, at Asher's birth—though there had been a disconcerting mix-up: he'd expected to find a baby wrapped in a blanket in the warmer, but walked into the hospital room to find Asher still halfway inside his mother, his puny, wet head stuck like a rolled rug between her thighs. Claudine was gripping some kind of medical trapeze and grunting while the lady doctor—she turned out to be a midwife—crouched at the footboard; Asher's dark-haired scalp kept appearing and disappearing while Jimmy stood at the head of the bed, holding on to the post and mumbling illogical directions about breathing. Kleinman had taken a place just inside and to the left of the door (Camp Blanding, 1944, house-to-house maneuvers: MacArthur had been planning the invasion of Japan) and watched his own flesh and blood, once-removed, come out into the world.

But since then, somehow, he'd been afraid.

Of what? He and Ginger had had three of their own. Harry was in Texas now, a vice-provost at Rice University; Hannah was in California, teaching high school. But until this year there had been no grandchildren. An oddity of the modern period. Jimmy was forty by now, and at that age Kleinman had already had two children in high school. And Ginger had never lost her beauty, not even after three; no, it had actually grown—a splendid, flowering vine! A radiance! (If she were here now, he wouldn't be afraid.) What did you say to a baby? He'd never had her gift, had never known how to counter their blank expressions, their wet-lipped stares, their illogical grunts and offerings. But that was silly. It's an instinct, he told himself. See what happens.

No, Jimmy was *fifty!*—or near to it: that's right! He remembered now. Born the year the B-50 circled the globe. A long time ago, but you don't forget how to raise a child. It would come back to him. Another memory: holding a bottle for Jimmy, sitting next to the Allegheny River as a locomotive rumbled over the trestle bridge above. Nineteen fifty, and the striking railroads were being run by the U.S. Army. Wondering if his business was going to survive. Watching a man drink beer on a flatboat. That was all he could think of, though. Ginger had done the rest.

~~~~~~~~~~~~~~~~~~~~~~~~~~~~~~~~~~~~~

If he'd had a refrain in his life it would have been this: Take the advice of no one. It was an almost effortless credo, although the irony of it as a dictum was not lost upon him either. The one who'd given him this counsel was his mother, and she gave it to him over and over. In April 1932, she was the young wife of the middle-aged owner of a successful linen mill in Hamburg, Germany, when Paul von Hindenburg defeated Adolf Hitler for the presidency of the Weimar Republic. Kleinman's grandfather Morris Gertzmann, who had founded the mill, and his father, Isaac Gertzmann, a finely dressed, scornful man who was poised to inherit it, rejoiced that von Hindenburg's election marked the end for the National Socialists, and they spent the evening toasting the turn in events. The Gertzmann house, a three-parapeted stone mansion that overlooked the Herrengraben canal, half a mile from the Elbe, was thrown open to friends and business associates of the family, and three young female conservatory students were brought in to perform Schubert lieder. August was ten years old. The Gertzmanns were quite prominent in Hamburg, and in their house were fine paintings, statues of Italian marble, and a collection of stringed instruments from the Cremonese makers of the seventeenth century. His father had a Domenico Montagnana cello, although he didn't know how to play it, and both a François Tourte and a Dominique Peccatte bow. Usually he allowed the hired musicians to perform only on copies of the bows, which he had had fabricated for this purpose, and kept the originals in a cast-iron fire box behind a false panel above the rear staircase; but tonight he produced the genuine articles and after several snifters of brandy even stepped up onto the low stage himself and added his poorly aimed baritone to the lieder.

From down the hall, August listened to his father's thick voice. Not only had he always felt invisible in his father's presence, but he had always been clumsy around revelry; now, while the business acquaintances inside toasted, laughed, and made appraising remarks about the musicians, August walked out onto the short iron balcony that hung from the end of the hallway over the misty waters of the canal. There, his mother soon joined him. For some time, she too had been living in the Gertzmann house in a state of isolation. She stepped to the rail and gazed up and down the dark waterway. Then she pointed up at the stone façade behind them, where burning lamps cast their orange light all the way to the peaked turrets of her husband's study. They could see guests at every level of the edifice. "Nobody else thinks it's worth wasting any oil on von Hindenburg," she said to August, pointing down the dark canal toward the Elbe. "Only your naïve father."

Several months later, when Hitler was appointed chancellor, Isaac Gertzmann again assured his family that von Hindenburg would control the situation. Again there were festivities, though this time nearly all the guests at dinner were Jews. A string quartet was brought in, but no singer, and the music was limited to Brahms and Mozart. August's mother had taken to reading the *Völkischer Beobachter* in secret, because her husband would not allow it into the house, and that evening she read it aloud to August. He did not understand its content but was aware that his father forbade it because it had become an organ of the National Socialists. This is why his mother subscribed. "Take the advice of no one," she told him that night, reading to him, as he lay in bed, from an editorial on *die Judenfrage*. Downstairs, the quartet was still playing, and he could hear the clink of his father's snifters on the marble end tables. "And know your enemy," she added.

~~~~~~~~~~~~~~~~~~~~~~~~~~~~~~~~~~

Walking up the front path to Jimmy's building, Kleinman took a yarmulke from his back pocket and set it on his head. It wouldn't stay in place: maybe God knew. Since boyhood, yarmulkes had never stayed—something about the shape of his cranium: an irreligious skull. He still had plenty of hair, though—thank his mother's father for that. He laughed and pushed the yarmulke down on the crown again. He was trying to start off on the right foot with Claudine. He wished he had a bobby pin. Clean his teeth with it and then get the yarmulke to stay in place: a pleasing efficiency. The door opened and Claudine, who he was fairly sure was Catholic, said, "Good Shabbes."

"That's 'Good *yontif*,' " Kleinman answered.

"No it's not," she said. "It can be 'Good Shabbes,' too."

"*Yontif* is for a holiday," Kleinman said. "Shabbes is only for the Sabbath, which is tomorrow."

"Take a peek at the calendar, Pop," said Jimmy. "The Sabbath is today."

Kleinman had a calendar on his watch, but he didn't look at it. When Claudine opened her arms, he was glad to step into them. How the hell was that possible?—a whole day gone! How could today be Saturday? What had he done? He patted her shoulder blades as a signal of release, but she seemed willing to hug him as long as he wanted to stand there. "Robinson Crusoe," he said when he felt his face was no longer red. "Didn't he lose the Sabbath?" He turned toward Jimmy.

"Yeah," said Jimmy, his hand out. "But he was on a desert island."

"And so is your father, I guess," said Kleinman.

"How'd you get all wet, Grandpa Augie?" said Claudine.

"The cab broke down. I had to walk. Now," said Kleinman, "I want to see your baby boy."

They went straight upstairs to the nursery, where Asher was asleep, still looking like a creature of water. Kleinman bent over the bassinet. Didn't really feel anything. No memories. "Oh," he said. "I forgot. I have a present in the car." He turned for the door.

"Pop, you can get it later."

"No, no. I picked it up especially."

But on the sidewalk he suddenly realized: maybe he'd forgotten to take it from the cab. Lord, not again. He checked the front seat. He checked the back. They were going to think he had gone foggy. It occurred to him there might be a toy store nearby; he could drive there and be back in no time. Finally, he found it in the trunk. When had he put it there?

"It's beautiful," Claudine said upstairs, lifting it from the box. "And it's perfect for his age."

"Hey, you don't raise three of them yourself and not learn something."

"The lady at the toy store helped you, Pop," Jimmy said. "You don't fool me."

Asher woke up.

"Look, pumpkin," said Claudine. "Little fish! Little hanging fish from your grandpa!"

"There're animals too," Kleinman said. "Look, a sheep. A cow. A camel."

"We can hang it over the crib," Claudine said. "Here, why don't you hold him?"

"That's a llama," said Jimmy, "not a camel."

"He looks comfortable where he is," said Kleinman.

"No, he wants to go in his grandpa's arms. Don't you, pumpkin?"

"Let me take off my coat first."

But Claudine had already picked him up in his blanket. Then he was in Kleinman's arms, a stunned fish in a net. The sleeves of Kleinman's overcoat were slippery; he gripped hard. In truth, he had expected something heavier. This baby felt like nothing at all, the lightness itself difficult to hold. He could almost not feel him there in his hands. He had a sudden memory: carrying his baby brother, Izzy, in the flaps of his winter coat, walking in the ocean bite of the Rockaway winter.

Jimmy was watching him curiously. He pulled a Kleenex from the box.

"What is that?" said Kleinman.

Jimmy let his hand fall.

"Here," Claudine said. "Do it like this."

"Right," he said. "That did feel a little wrong. It's been a long time."

"That's right—one hand there, like that. Good. They like to be bounced."

"Your husband always liked to be bounced, too," said Kleinman.

"He still does," Claudine said.

Kleinman laughed. Jimmy didn't.

The problem of money. Kleinman had done what this country had allowed him to—preposterous wealth by any reasonable measure, fortune upon fortune, exorbitant reward for five years of boldness and a half century of diligence. Yet years ago he had become most keenly aware of the inequity of his lucre: no dark coal mines for him, no fine industrial dust choking his lungs. In business he had always paid better than the going wage, seen to any man who fell ill, in the flush years sent surprise checks in the mail, and at Thanksgiving dressed in a canvas-and-leather Pilgrim's outfit—what a holiday! what a country!—and handed out whole turkeys to his employees. But then his life had turned, a bleak last chapter that had come upon him as pure surprise, and he was forced for the first time in decades to reflect upon his pecuniary motivations. They had, in fact, vanished. He had three different brokers who called him at home now, apparently just to chat, but he no longer cared to talk with any of them. His attentions lay elsewhere.

Charity was easy. He gave to the Guttmacher Institute, the United Negro College Fund, the Carnegie Museum of Art, the ACLU, Amnesty International, and the children's hospitals in Pittsburgh, Philadelphia, and now Boston. And he sent a good-sized check every year to a monkish man he had heard about who was building clinics for the poor in the West Indies. Solicitations arrived in the mail, and each Friday evening at his desk he sorted through them, acceding to nearly every request. What else was there to spend it on? He favored a sandwich shop in Cambridge that for six dollars served a Reuben the size of an overshoe. That was the only meal he needed in a day. His walls were already thick with art. He owned two weeks' worth of suits, a reliable Lincoln, a mattress from Sweden, a walking stick—never used—of mahogany, pearl, and smuggled Angolan ivory. It rested in his closet.

In front of him, the world was changing. Even a man of his solitary circumstances could not be unaware of this. His window looked onto the corner of Gloucester and Newbury: German cars, young men ordering cellared wines in the cafés, telephones in shirt pockets. His own wealth was significant—but no longer, he understood, rare. And what was this new state of affairs going to do for the world? Sometimes on the street he watched faces—cops, bums, tycoons—looking for clues. Where on the scale of fortune did the human soul flower? Work was the satisfying thing, he knew, discipline superior to possession. Yet all around him the money was being spent like madness itself, a torrid clamor for justification. The vine was bearing its bloom, a brazen, oversweet flower. Or was the true justification merely fear? This he could understand. Since childhood he himself had feared ruin. Feared it everywhere. Feared it for his mother first; then later for his wife, then his children; feared it for himself. Feared it every day, while in the shadow of his fear he had gathered a fortune. Now everything had changed. The fear was gone. Ruin had appeared, but from a different direction entirely. That was the irony. When panhandled, he gave out twenty-dollar bills.

A ll right," Jimmy said suddenly at lunch. "I'll get to the point. We think it's time you moved back to New York. Moved closer to us. What's Boston? Boston's nothing to you."

"Why the sudden interest?"

"Pop, you're not getting any younger."

Claudine said, "We'd thought at least you might like to stay an extra night. Not go home Monday. Stay till Tuesday, or maybe Wednesday. Give yourself some time to see what it's like here. At least do that. It was Jimmy's idea."

They were eating tuna sandwiches, too dry for Kleinman's taste. "Why doesn't Jimmy ask me, then?"

"How about it, Pop?"

Kleinman paused. "I'll have to think," he answered.

Claudine burst out laughing.

"What's so funny?"

"You! Of course. Of course you want to stay. Anybody can see it! You can be with your grandson."

"He might have business," said Jimmy.

"What business?" Claudine said. "At Bread and Circus?"

"How did you know about Bread and Circus?" said Kleinman.

"A little bird told me."

"What's Bread and Circus?" said Jimmy.

"I'm honored that you would ask an old man to stay," Kleinman answered.

"Good," Claudine said. "You can baby-sit. And you can think about moving down here permanently. By the way, Jimmy," she said, picking up Asher. "I think he needs to burp."

"What's Bread and Circus?"

"Why don't you show your father how to burp him?"

"What's Bread and Circus, Pop?"

"Your father is employed at the Bread and Circus Corporation," Kleinman said sharply.

"You're what?"

"I'm a bagger of groceries."

Jimmy stopped eating.

"What do you want me to do? Become a docent at the museum?"

"Why are you doing that?"

"Because I like to, that's why. I see people all day. And I do my job well."

"I don't believe it."

"What's not to believe?"

"See," Claudine said. "You should move down here, be closer to us. If you want to work, you can baby-sit—be with your own flesh and blood." She touched her blouse above her heart. "So, will you stay the extra night?"

Kleinman set down his coffee. "Well, that's very kind of you."

"It's not kind," said Claudine. "It's a pleasure for us, too. And for Asher."

"You mean those are the only two choices?" Jimmy said. "Docent or grocery clerk? Are you lifting heavy bags, Pop?"

"Caveat emptor," Kleinman said. "I haven't baby-sat in forty years!"

"Nothing's changed," Claudine answered. "Jimmy, why don't you burp this little one while I clear?"

"You better not be lifting anything heavy, Pop."

"Thank you for the invitation," said Kleinman. "But unfortunately I'll have to come back. I'm going out of town next week."

"You are?" Jimmy said. "Where?"

Kleinman added milk to his coffee and sipped it. Actually, he wasn't going out of town at all. For some time he had been contemplating a trip, but he had never made plans. "None of your concern," he answered.

"Come on, Pop. It certainly is our concern."

"All right, then. I'll tell you." He sipped his coffee. "I'm going to the island of Honshu."

"What?"

"It's in Japan."

"How wonderful," said Claudine.

"Thank you."

"God almighty," said Jimmy.

Claudine Bishop was a good ten years younger than Jimmy and had converted for him shortly before they were married. This had been a surprise, perhaps the largest of Kleinman's life. What did Jimmy care who was Jewish! But there had been all the rituals and obligations of a conversion, arcane and insensible in the modern world. At every level, discouragement from the rabbi; a course of study; a questioning; a bath. It was preposterous.

A month before the wedding, Claudine's parents had come to meet August and Ginger. This was eight years ago. Pleasant enough people. But he was the caretaker or something, the horse breeder (was that it?) on a gentleman's farm in Virginia. A horse breeder! (Kleinman's first thought: *Cossacks!*) A gentleman's farm in Virginia! The whole family had the high, optimistic facial bones of some northern tribe, the Scottish perhaps; red-cheeked and full of conversation, all of them. Usually a quiet man married a garrulous woman, or vice versa; this was something Kleinman and everyone else in the world had noticed. But not so with the Bishops! Claudine talked; her father talked; her mother talked. They all seemed to be excited by the prospect of Judaism (already a misunderstanding, Kleinman thought). Perhaps they would convert too! Kleinman had excused himself and gone to the kitchen, poured himself a Glenfiddich, and stared at the daguerreotype of his own father as a boy, scowling alongside the Elbe River next to a horse cart full of linen.

The truth was, Jimmy himself practically needed to convert. He knew nothing of Judaism. There'd been not a lick of it in their household. Ginger had been a Catholic (the defining difficulty of his life—but he'd do it again in an instant!), and Kleinman's stepfather, after a point, had essentially given up on offering him a religious education—not exactly disavowing him, but simply leaving him to climb away alone, as though over the high, dirty walls of the shtetl. Kleinman didn't blame him: he could see the anguish of his stepfather's natural sociability at war with his religious sanctity. There was a great deal of pain in this distancing, which his mother, in his later opinion, had been forced to follow; but in the world of breweries and beer distribution, Judaism would have been a chain rattling around his ankle. And he'd been glad of an excuse to be rid of it. There'd been no religion to speak of in his house. No Christmas (a commercial invasion of the family!). No Chanukah (just a reaction to Christmas!). No candles. No bar mitzvahs. No nothing. It had driven his parents from him, but in fact it had given his own wife and children more time together with him as human beings. On Friday nights Ginger played the piano for them, then they all went to the movies; and on Sunday mornings they rode bicycles to the park or to the promenade along the Allegheny River.

But somehow something had persisted in this one son. Perhaps it was purely a matter of Gertzmann genetics. Jimmy had Ginger's Neapolitan nose and the clear reminder in his cheeks of the sheer falls of bone that accentuated her comely mouth; yet still he had inherited the unmistakable dominance of Kleinman's paternal blood. The persistent youthfulness of the cheeks, which shone in cold weather like slices of ham; the broad, piscine lips; the feminine hands, too delicate for labor, that belied an obdurate character. It was as though the genes themselves were as obstinate as the people. Unquestionably a Gertzmann, though diluted. In truth, when Jimmy was in his thirties, the resemblance had been of studied interest to Kleinman, who, for a few sorrowful months after the death of his mother, had woken sometimes at night to wonder about his own paternal lineage.

And then somehow, in his forties, Judaism, a religion of which he had not even technically been a member, had become essential to Jimmy. And he had asked Claudine to go along with him as well. Kleinman had to laugh. It was as though now the Gentiles suddenly felt *sorry* for them; or perhaps it was that as a people it was now the goyim's turn to rebel, the way his generation of New York–born had dropped the -steins and -mans from their names and come across the bridges into Manhattan. That was the way the world bumped along. Kleinman's stepfather had worn a tallith and tefillin, made them daven on the Sabbath at sundown. Kleinman could still recall the mothy smell of the prayer shawl and the tang of candle smoke in the salt-misted Rockaway evenings. It had been for the sake of his own children, he had told himself a half-century ago, coming to speak to the priest with Ginger, that he had finally thrown off the yoke.

~~~~~~~~~~~~~~~~~~~~~~~~

A s soon as he returned to Boston, he called the travel agent and told her to arrange the trip: he wanted to leave in two days. Autumn was in the air. The mornings brought inland the coppery taste of the Charles, and within him he felt the acute pressure of time such as he had never before known. His children wanted him to live in New York again: he knew in the end he would not resist. And the sheet from Dr. Stern was still in his wallet, though he had been reassured that the diagnosis was merely a warning; it changed nothing. When the travel agent told him the price of a first-class ticket, he chuckled for her benefit, then said, "You're kidding me, are you not?"

"Not kidding at all, Mr. Kleinman."

He demurred then, suspecting graft, and walked to another agency. But there they told him the same thing. "This is short notice, Mr. Kleinman," said the agent. "Such freedom costs money."

"Freedom?" said Kleinman. "This isn't freedom. It's obligation."

"Fine."

The mahogany frame was still perfectly sealed—he had to visit the hardware store for a straight-blade before he was able to pry away the backing, and then make a second trip for needle-nose pliers when he discovered there were dozens of tiny brads embedded in the wood. At an art-supply store on Newbury Street he bought a small leather portfolio for carrying the letter, at the Boston Public Library he checked out a five-year-old guidebook to Honshu, and at Filene's he found a sturdy carry-on bag with wheels—they all had wheels now, he noted: a shame he hadn't invented that fifty years ago. From the refrigerator he took the bulbs and nestled them in the pocket of his sport coat, inside their velvet sack. On the dining room table he left instructions for his lawyer in case anything happened. He was only going to be away for four days. As an afterthought, he went down to the basement, found the burlap sack, and laid it flat at the bottom of the carry-on. He packed a wrinkle-proof raincoat, a change of underwear, a bottle of Dramamine, and the guidebook. He wanted to travel light. In first class, he remembered, they gave you a toiletry kit. The portfolio he would carry with him on board.

O ne morning in the spring of 1933, his mother showed him an item in the *Völkischer Beobachter*, and that evening, after Isaac Gertzmann had retired to his study to review his accounts, she dressed August in his oilskin coat and went out with him by carriage toward Kaiser-Friedrich-Ufer, along the Laebek canal. It was mid-May, and though the tulips were blooming in orderly rows along the housefronts, the night air still bore the prickly chill of a Hamburg winter. Several blocks away from any businesses, his mother relieved the coachman to wait for them, and in their hats and long coats she and August set out on foot toward the commercial district. They came out onto a square along the water. The streets were dark, but in one corner of the plaza a small group of figures had gathered. She pulled August along next to her, and they arrived a few doors down from the activity just as a torch was lit. Men were tossing books onto a pallet that had been propped above the storm drain. Every few minutes another load of books would arrive in a handcart from around the corner, and the men would toss them onto the heap, which was already the size of a grand piano. There were some older boys there, too, whom August recognized from the Gymnasium, and they seemed to be looking through the volumes and taking some off the pile to read. There were no more than a dozen people in the square.

At 11 P.M. his mother pointed up to the clock tower and said, "Now, watch this—I wish your father was here to see it." They heard a rumble, and then from around the corner a motorcycle with a sidecar appeared; a man disembarked, said a few words to the others, and stepped to the front of the pile. Turning to the small group of onlookers in the doorways, he called out, "*Wir müssen den Kampf ansagen, allem, was uns hemmt, so zu sein, wie wir müssen!*" A photographer was there with a tripod, and a sodium lamp flashed. Then the man retrieved a can from the motorcycle sidecar, poured its contents over the books, removed the torch from its stand, and lit the pile on fire.

It blazed upward, roaring. The few onlookers gasped. August's mother took his hand, and they made their way back through the misty alleyways to where the coach awaited them. "Just in case you didn't know," she said. "Those were Jewish books."

The following morning there was an item on the front page of the *Hamburger Morgenpost*, but Isaac Gertzmann scoffed. "How many people were there?" he said to his wife. He tugged at both his earlobes. "The paper says fifteen."

"That's about right," she responded. "I saw one of Heinz Liepmann's books in the pile."

"Fifteen vagrants do not constitute a movement," he said curtly. "And if this Liepmann is one of those triflers you read, then they have done us all a service." Isaac Gertzmann was a brooding, illiberal man, invariably angry in the morning, who had long made August feel that he and his mother were one family, the Gertzmanns another. He reached to ladle gooseberry preserves onto his bread. Then he tugged again at both his earlobes. "Besides," he sniffed, returning to the newspaper. "This is not some Abyssinian hut village. This is Hamburg!"

"Pop," Jimmy said. "It's a ridiculous idea. What's in Japan that's not in Boston?"

"I've just always wanted to go."

"It's not ridiculous," said Claudine. "It's wonderful. I hope I'm like you when I get to be your age."

Jimmy laughed.

"What's so funny about that?" Claudine said.

"Sweetheart, my father's never gone anywhere on vacation in his life. What are you really going to do there, Pop? You're making some kind of business deal, aren't you?"

"Young man, you will remember I took your mother to Barbados."

Jimmy was silent.

"What part of Honshu are you going to see?" said Claudine.

"Some small towns in the hills."

"You're kidding us, right, Pop?"

"I'm not kidding you in the least."

"Why there?" said Claudine.

"I have a few things to do."

"Well, that's a long flight, Pop. Why don't you at least go business class?"

"What?" said Kleinman. "Are you kidding? Coach is fine for an old mutt like me."

"Jimmy always flies first class," said Claudine.

"Claudine honey, that's not at all true."

"Yes, it is. That's what you always tell me."

"My son likes to be comfortable."

"That's because I upgrade. I don't pay for it." He rose from the table. As a boy, when his brother, Harry, teased him, he used to rise the same way, turning away from all of them. "And, Pop," he said. "You know, you should tell us when you're planning to go out of town."

"I'm telling you now."

"You should tell us a little more in *advance*," said Jimmy. "And if we hadn't asked, you would never have mentioned it."

"I didn't want to worry you."

"You wouldn't worry us, Pop. But what if something happened?"

"You could have called me in Japan."

Claudine started to laugh.

"They have phones there, too, you know," Kleinman said. "And here's a surprise—they're even better than ours. That's what I've read. Everyone has one of those pocket phones, every single person. Even out in the country—what's so funny, may I ask?"

"I meant," said Jimmy, "what if something happened to *you*—"

"Shhh," Claudine said. "That was so sweet." She moved behind Kleinman, and on the top of his head he felt either the touch of her hand or a kiss. This girl threw him for a loop. "Now," she said. "What about burping this little one? Show your father, sweetie, how nothing's changed."

On the first of June, 1933, August was awakened by his mother in the middle of the night. He was told to dress in warm clothes, though summer had already arrived, and to pack what he could fit into a narrow leather duffel that she handed to him when he rose from bed. She disappeared upstairs while August moved quietly around the house packing his items, and when she returned, they went out onto the balcony. A fine mist was in the air. Below them on the black canal, a covered yawl was moored, and from beneath its oilcloth tarp a man appeared and handed up a tradesman's ladder. The yawl was carrying barrels of pitch, and when the tarp was lifted for their entrance, it let loose a startling discharge of ammonia and heat. A pile of other tarps was stacked at one end of the deck, and before they sat down and covered themselves, his mother handed August a pearl necklace and an alabaster brooch and told him to hide them in his boots. She handed something to the pilot, who then took his place mid-boat at the oarlocks. August watched his mother's face, looking for fear; but there was none. So he felt none himself: they might have been sneaking out for a picnic. Soon he grew accustomed to the acrid smell, and he lay down and closed his eyes. He had always loved his mother, deeply, painfully, in part as recompense for the dismissals both of them had suffered at the hands of his father and in part because they were so obviously of the same blood; and now, as they crept downstream accompanied by the rhythmic pull and pause of the boatman's oar strokes, he felt that at last he was going to be alone with her. For eternity, he found himself thinking. The smell of the pitch had become rather pleasant—it had a sweet undertone of burning wood—and before long, waves could be heard slapping on the hull. They had reached the Elbe.

From there they went up a gangway into the hold of a ship, where they spent that day and night on hard cots in a small, dark cabin without good air. They must have been near the engine room, for the walls rumbled ceaselessly, as though an unending train were passing across the ceiling. Still, miraculously, he felt no fear, and was not sorry at all that they had left his father behind. The following morning a sailor came for them, speaking in rudimentary German, and when they emerged above-ship, August sensed land to the right of them, enshrouded in fog. The engines quieted when a tug came alongside, and then he heard the sound of breakers. Suddenly they were through the fog, and cliffs appeared above. For the rest of his life he could not look at a picture of those cliffs, the chalky bluffs of Dover, without tears coming to his eyes. A month later, in Hamburg, his father and grandfather were beaten to death by a mob who had been let in by the police through the locked doors of the Gertzmann linen mill.

Kleinman did not learn this, of course, until almost two years later, when a letter from the mill's linen dyer, who had been employed by the Gertzmanns since childhood, was read to him by his mother in Wavecrest, in the borough of Queens, where the two of them had gone to live. They had passed by train from Dover to Bristol, where his mother had a cousin, spent a month there, and then found passage to New York on a vessel carrying crates of ball bearings and a few well-off refugees, arranged by a violin dealer to whom August, with the consent of his mother, had sold the counterfeit Peccatte bow.

~~~~~~~~~~~~~~~~~~~~~~~~

In Narita Airport, at the gaijin customs booth, the agent studied his disembarkation card. Under "Purpose," Kleinman had written *pleasure*; though, if he had been conscientious about it, he might have written *duty*, or, strangely, *justice*. An extraordinary thought for him that after all the events of his life, which he now thought of broadly as the Flight, the Battle, the Riches, and the Decline, he should feel thus compelled. That he should believe there was any such thing as justice was to his current mind, as he stood waiting for the agent to flip through the pages of his passport, incongruous. How is there justice for his father and grandfather, dead without graves in Hamburg? For Ginger, stricken when she was, as years of plenty stood before them? For himself, whose life after Ginger was a punctured vessel, filled vainly by a job and music and now trips? He might have written *recompense*. But there was a romantic side to himself that he was now discovering as well. No, not romantic. *Mystic. Reverent.*

"Pleasure?" the agent said.

"Yes."

The man smiled. "Four days in Japan is few."

It seemed like a pleasantry until Kleinman realized he was being interrogated. "*Directed* pleasure," he said in response, and his own subtle smile was from the delight of such jousting—he remembered the feeling from selling luggage. Yet he was prepared to say no more. The tulip bulbs were still in the pocket of his coat—he was not sure of the legality of such conveyance, but if the agent had questioned him further, sent him off into one of the shorter lines in which the occasional traveler stood for more thorough investigation, he would have shrugged perhaps and abandoned his plans, waited in the airport for the next flight back to Logan. This was what his life had distilled itself to—a contest of mysticism and pragmatics. Now pragmatics was surging. He was wondering about the portfolio in his carry-on—if he was asked to open it, he would have to tell them something else about his visit.

But the agent questioned him no further. He smiled again and sent him through, and Kleinman emerged into an atrium above the luggage area, larger than any he'd ever seen, filled, like a dark lake, with men in black suits. There were signs everywhere, but all of them were in Japanese. He descended the escalator and looked around for someone he might recognize from his flight. The men were uniformly dressed and difficult to tell apart—he would recognize one, then see another, and begin to doubt his judgment; the women were infrequent. Some of the older men, no doubt, had been on the same islands he had, fifty years ago, peering out of the jungle.

At the foot of the escalator he stood, unsure of what to do, parting a stream of commerce that opened before him and then closed behind. A bit of dizziness came, and he moved to the wall. What in God's name had he gotten himself into? How would he even get to Sounzan? And how would he find an old lady there whose name he only partially knew? Then a young woman approached, and it was not until she stood immediately to his side that he realized she was holding up a card stenciled with his name. He felt faint with relief. "Dr. Livingstone, I presume," he said.

"Oh," she answered. "Very sorry."

"Wait, wait," he said, taking her elbow. "Just a joke. That's me,

August Kleinman. You got the right fellow. You understand me, right? How did you know I was coming? How'd you spot me in this crowd?"

"Welcome to Japan," she answered. She emitted a tiny laugh, like a bee flying out of her mouth, then covered her lips.

"Oh, I see," Kleinman said. "The travel agent arranged this. CityWide Travel arranged this?"

"I am for take you to Capitol Tokyu Hotel."

Kleinman said, "So, you speak good English?"

She laughed again. "Oh yes. Quite good."

"Then perhaps you can take me further than Tokyo. I am going to Sounzan. Do you know Sounzan? I have to find some-one there. An old woman—that is, a woman my age. Can you take me?"

"Yes, of course," she said. She smiled. "She is your friend?" She giggled again.

"No," Kleinman said. "Not exactly. I'll tell you all about it if you want."

K leinman's new life bewildered him. This had occurred to him one day two years ago as he waited in the express line at the Bread & Circus on Prospect, an apple in his hand. He had always been a man of deeds, not the sort of person who enjoyed a life of leisure. But now, alone, everything once again seemed to be a test. He missed Ginger. In his accounts at A. G. Edwards, Mellon, and Smith Barney he had almost $12 million, but this treasure—though it had been his life, his entire life—meant nothing to him at all. The apple was 80 cents. He said, "There's been a mistake."

"How is that?" asked the cashier, whose name tag said ISABELA. She had black hair, eyes dark as stones.

"A dollar for an apple," he said. "That's a mistake."

"Eighty cents, not a dollar."

"An apple should be a nickel."

"And the streets should be safe for children."

She had Latin vowels but perfect English, a small flash of silver in her teeth when she smiled. Kleinman wanted her to keep talking. He laughed. "Yes," he said. "But for now we have the problem of the apple."

"I'll call my team leader if you'd like, sir."

"No, don't do that."

The man behind him—he was a lawyer, Kleinman could see: tailored gabardine pants, suspenders—said, "Sir, I'll buy you the apple."

"No thank you," said Kleinman.

"Look, old man. I'm in a hurry."

Kleinman said, "On second thought—yes, call the manager."

"For Chrissakes," said the lawyer.

"The lovely sound of your voice," Kleinman said to Isabela. "And your lovely name—where are you from?"

"Old man, there's a long line here, for Chrissakes."

"And you got behind a slow truck, young fella."

"The West Indies," said Isabela. The vowels flew from the tip of her tongue like seeds.

"Where in the West Indies?"

"The rudeness—" said a woman farther back in line.

"Sorry, everybody," Isabela said, smiling shyly.

Kleinman turned his back to the line. "I was there once," he said. "Ten years ago, I think it was. Beautiful. The west coast of Barbados. Which island are you from?"

"Christ almighty," said the lawyer. "I don't believe—"

"Very good," she said. "Most people here don't even know what the West Indies are."

Kleinman looked again: undoubtedly an intelligence behind the eyes. He took a hundred-dollar bill from his wallet.

The manager appeared. "Can I help you?"

"I'd like to apply for a job."

"For Chrissakes," the lawyer hissed, "I don't believe it. Don't hire the kook."

Kleinman set the hundred on the register. "There," he said to the lawyer. "It was worth your wait. Your groceries are paid for." He looked for the woman who'd called him rude. "Yours too," he said.

The manager said, "You're sure you need a job here?"

Kleinman said, "Dead sure."

The manager led him to the back, past an old man in line, who set his frozen dinner on the floor to clap for him. Kleinman bowed. In the rear office he was left at a linoleum desk, where he filled out the forms. Under "Experience," he wrote: *founded and ran the largest brewery in the state of Pennsylvania and eleventh largest in the United States.* For "Age," he considered his options, then wrote: *61.* Under "Available hours," he wrote: *all.*

The manager came back in and looked over his sheet. "Why do you want to be part of the Bread and Circus team?"

"That's a reasonable question," Kleinman said. "But what does it matter?"

"Pardon?"

"Life is for the living," Kleinman said. "A gift. I'm bored."

"We emphasize customer service here. That's the Bread and Circus way."

"And mine too, incidentally. That's how I built my business."

"We start with a trial period. Make sure you fit in with your service team, and vice versa, of course. Three weeks."

"Just give me my helmet, coach."

The manager didn't smile. "When can you start?"

"I'd like to work when Isabela works."

"We work in service teams here."

"Then put me on her team."

"Hold on a second," he said. He disappeared through the door. Several minutes passed. Inside the desk drawer was a Cross pen in an inlaid wooden box. Kleinman used to do the same thing at the brewery: he looked around for the hidden camera. Finally, the manager returned. "Isabela says that's fine," he said. "When would you be available to start?"

"Yesterday," Kleinman answered.

~~~~~~

H is life, it seemed to him, could be arranged like a set of mountains in the desert—an expanse of flat, then suddenly a peak. Or perhaps this was only the result of how his memory now worked: long, trundling periods of obscurity broken randomly by jags of startling recollection. The years in Hamburg were reduced in his mind to a few blurred semblances: the long avenues and the converted coal carriage on which at each stop his father's manager sat silently in his bowler holding a pocket watch in his hand, waiting for August to cart the bolts of linen; the crescendo of a string quartet downstairs in the house on Herrengraben; the light from the burning books illuminating a carved gargoyle on an iron-gated postern on Kaiser-Friedrich-Ufer. Then the flight with his mother, which he could reproduce with exactitude in his mind: the pull and lull of the boatman's oars, the smell of pitch, the rumbling of the ship's screw, the cliffs in fog at Dover. Then the Rockaways, the oppressive talk of his new uncles, who were in the meat business, and his aunts, who competed over inventing new ways to reuse everything—milk caps, newspaper ties, sprung clothespins—and discussed it like gemologists. This, too, blurred. The days and days in a classroom at P.S. 106 while English grew comfortable on his tongue. At nineteen came the war: December 7, 1941—he was a senior at Far Rockaway High, reading about Bruiser Kinard against the Green Bay Packers, the radio playing his mother's music in the background, a seagull alighting on the lamppost and turning to look in the window at him—as though it understood there was news—just as the announcer broke into the program. Jascha Heifetz playing the Mendelssohn violin concerto, then Japanese bombers striking the U.S.S. *Arizona* on the island of Oahu. Two years later Kleinman stepped off the train in Camp Blanding, Florida, for basic training, onto a platform where he heard a couple of officers, not quite under their breath, say, "Jew boy." He could hear it to this day: the elegant, genteel vowels.

This was 1944. The Marshall Islands had fallen quickly to the Allies, and rumors were in the barracks of the battles that would come before the assault on the Japanese mainland. At Camp Blanding they received their basic training from a nasty-mouthed, sunburned Cajun as tall as a giant, who tortured them for four months and seemed to enjoy it—then, on the morning they left, shook each of their hands with tears in his eyes. They were headed for the Far East—that was all Kleinman knew, and even this was unconfirmed. A week later they crossed through the Panama Canal at dawn on a Liberty Ship, bound for San Francisco Bay, and after a day of shore leave there, which Kleinman spent reading a William Saroyan novel at the foot of Coit Tower, they were again at sea, in the midst of a convoy that disappeared over the horizon, this time headed for the South Pacific. Destroyers rode the periphery, but his own ship was a rusting merchant-marine cargo hauler, painted gray and refitted with bunks bolted four high onto the walls. The Jap was a vicious enemy worse than the Hun. There was no surrender in the Jap code of war. That was the talk on board. Old women asking for water carried rifles in their robes. The fallen lay atop booby-trapped artillery shells, waiting for the GI medics.

Eight days out to sea, though, the water was calm as a pond, the war a threat that somehow had never materialized; the sun warm above deck, the men at ease. His unit was a mix—Jews and Italians from the boroughs, Southern Baptists, quiet boys from New England farms. They played cards, watched the featureless horizon. Then on the ninth day, while they sat playing draw poker in the high afternoon sun, there came a sound like a giant steel ball hitting the water; half a mile back a destroyer rolled to starboard and went down. The zigzagging started, and the fighting ships went into gear. Night fell and another boat took a hit; Kleinman heard the news below deck, where he was having his first experiences with fear. An enemy submarine was working the periphery. By morning word came that it had been destroyed, but now the fear was in him and he knew—right then, the ship's engines rattling, the zigzagging and the fear causing all the men to vomit, one by one—that he could never be the same.

It took them another week to reach their destination, a makeshift tent camp in the deep jungle near Rockhampton, in northeast Australia, where for another two months they lived inside the stinking, shrieking thicket, half in the dark, training in survival and attack, and awaited their orders. Disease crept in among the crowded cots: rotting nails, sanguineous ulcers, worms that entered through the feet if one walked barefoot through the mud to the showers. Dysentery struck nearly everyone, and vines were used for suspenders to hold up the sagging trousers. Some of the worst off were shipped back out to the coast, where at least the sun would shine on their sores. Yet Kleinman, tougher than most, did not sicken; he became an excellent marksman and gained a certain respect among the unit for his assurance during their live-fire drills, although in his own mind it was nothing more than fatalism.

Finally, in the spring of 1945, their assignment came: an island beachhead near Okinawa, in the East China Sea. Rumors were passed of brutal losses. On a rainy evening they boarded ship, all the men quiet; the following night, somewhere east of Fuzhou, China, they were roused in the dark amid the roar of a terrible surf and loaded by ropes into landing craft. One by one the vessels approached the ship, where the soldiers climbed down into them like rats on the woven ladders; then they churned off into the darkness while the next wave of men climbed overboard and moved down toward the black water. On the ropes, Kleinman felt outside of his own life, the warm salt breeze filling him with his childhood memory of Hank Kleinman and the great sea at the Rockaways. Then he was down inside the long craft, the men standing shoulder to shoulder behind the high metal walls, checking their rifles, tightening their helmets. The deck pitched sternward, then leveled out and began to settle evenly into the rollers as the basin filled with soldiers. They pulled away, and the motors shifted to a higher pitch—they were moving at good speed now, aiming the landing toward the eastern shore so that the sun would rise behind them. To the rear, the troopship had disappeared. Above the walls the moon was shining through a hole in the clouds, and the men were cursing the bright night, stamping their feet on the pitched deck like horses. On the downward roll of a wave Kleinman glimpsed the beach, a pale crescent eight hundred yards ahead, no bombardment lighting it anywhere. Huge waves were breaking well out to sea—a reef must have surrounded the island. Suddenly, in their draw, Kleinman's craft lost power and instantly began to heave in the crashing swells; the steel walls rose over them, hurtling the men against one another, then dropped away as the GIs near the slanted mouth began pounding on the sides to get out; some tried to climb over the rim into the towering breakers; they were shouting to the other boats moving past; Kleinman prepared to swim, but then the engines caught again and the deck straightened. Then they were through the break, speeding inland, and finally the hull brushed bottom and pushed up the sloping approach to land. The door swung down and for a moment the sea air and the wash of the warm water on his legs were the greatest relief Kleinman had ever known. He held his Garand over his head and ran for shore.

But there was no fire from the beach, just the moon rising over a line of jungle and a string of toppled concrete bunkers in the shadows like rented bungalows in Edgemere. He dug in and fired, but soon GIs were standing and walking up the slope toward the trees. A man next to him lit a cigarette, and though the ember glowed like a beacon, Kleinman didn't move away. He was in the East China Sea in firing position on the dunes and still the war wasn't real.

At sunrise they marched up the beach to where a camp of Quonsets already stood at the mouth of a small river delta choked with sand. The coast, they learned, had been secured days ago.

The men who had arrived ahead of them had a look in their eyes, but Kleinman's unit ignored it, ate the first meat they'd seen in a week, and joked about their island vacation. Nobody told them what the mission was or how long they would be there. A rumor circulated that they were actually on the southernmost tip of the Japanese mainland, but their sergeant shot this down. They were in the Ryukyu Islands, a long way from Tokyo, and despite how it looked, the war was a long way from over.

They began their patrols, gradually making a circumference of the shore, but none of them saw action. All they saw were GIs. A generally hilarious mood began to build, based on the belief that this was an easy break for them, but then on the third night on land, a Jap with a knife crawled into a tent down the line from Kleinman's own and slit the throats of two GIs. There were sentries all along the periphery and the Jap had gotten through anyway. This spooked the troops. Suddenly nobody could sleep. The Japs moved better in the jungle than the Americans, so on patrol the GIs approached the canopy from the periphery, ringing it in from the shore, making it smaller, hacking it with machetes and burning it with gasoline. Even the trees resisted flame, though, smoking sourly, the wet leaves sizzling. Now and then a Jap sniper took out a GI, sometimes after a patrol had been in place for hours. It was as though they were baiting the Americans, watching them from inside the black carapace of vegetation, waiting and waiting.

Now the fear was with Kleinman day and night. Men woke shouting in their tents; there was one near him who wept—he could hear it after lights-out. While still at sea he had learned a trick, that this gut-doubling fear could be turned, with the right approach, into rage. It had happened one morning, early, when they came above deck for calisthenics, out into the painfully bright mid-ocean sun, and suddenly the ship started swerving again, speeding and slowing. And the terror of the night spent below in the blackened bunk-rooms came surging out of him as murderous fury: if a Jap had appeared suddenly over the gangway, he would have disemboweled him with his hand-knife. That night as he sat below deck, the ship running quiet—this was the signal, they all knew, of another submarine picked up on sonar—his fear turned to rage. This, somehow, had allowed him to sleep. And now, on the island, it worked again. He woke in a rage, went to sleep in a rage; he was grateful for it.

They took patrols every day. His fifth morning on shore, at the edge of a clearing where the jungle had been cut back and burned, he saw his first enemy dead. Half a dozen corpses lay faceup in a shallow mud gully fifty yards ahead, each of them covered with some kind of shimmering black cloth. It was over a hundred degrees out, and when his squad approached the gully, the shimmering cloth lifted up from the corpses and flew away into the vegetation. They were warned about booby traps and mines, warned again never to take off their helmets. The jungle was quiet, but as though on cue that afternoon a man using his helmet to scoop stream water took a bullet in the back of the head. The rest of the squad emptied their rifles into the treetops, and a moment later, in the distance a Jap thudded unseen to the ground. It was pure terror, made Kleinman realize again that they were being watched. Every minute. He wondered if the sniper was still in there, having dropped a sandbag as decoy. Everything dripped: sap from the trees, the daily rain, the sweat inside his uniform. There were venomous snakes, too, that sprang down from the canopy. When the platoon re-emerged onto the beach that afternoon, heading back to camp, Kleinman saw another GI, a friendly Italian from the Bronx he'd met on board ship, stop next to one of the Jap corpses, pat the ground around it, then use his fist to ram the point of his knife into the mouth. Then he stood, placed something in his pocket, and moved on to the next corpse. From across a stream and a line of dunes, Kleinman watched. The Italian made his way down the line of corpses until, as he was leaning over one of them, he was blasted into the air. He came down in two pieces. Kleinman vomited, and then he and another GI carried the two pieces back to camp. Kleinman had the legs. In the pants pocket he found four gold teeth.

H e bit into the last of his pot roast at dinner and said, "Hmm, that wasn't bad at all." The light outside the dining room was still bright: Claudine had insisted they eat before sundown.

"You mean, not bad for a *Gentile*," she said.

"For anybody," said Kleinman.

"You're not a Gentile anymore," said Jimmy.

Kleinman said, "Yom Kipper is my favorite holiday."

"How can it be your favorite holiday?" said Claudine. "It's the Day of Atonement."

"Because it's a good day to get things done. The lines are shorter—all the Jews are in shul. Who needs to atone?"

Claudine said, "You don't really mean that."

"I certainly do. I've always gone to a movie on Yom Kipper," he said. "Never a line. I saw *The Sting* that way."

"It's Yom Kip-*pur*," Claudine said.

"What?"

"Yom Kip-*pur.*"

"I say Yom Kipper."

"That's what self-hating Jews say," she answered.

"Ha!" said Kleinman.

"It was old-world Jews trying to sound American. That's all it was."

"Wait a minute," said Kleinman. "Excuse me. How can you say something like that?"

"Because it's true."

Kleinman found another bite of the roast. There was definitely something he liked about this girl. "All right," he said. "Maybe you're right. But to me it doesn't matter. It's just a word. I wouldn't mind saying it your way. Yom Kip-*pur,*" he tried. He thought of Hank Kleinman, somehow, handing a nickel to the Sabbath goy to operate the staircase light for his mother. Then he burst out laughing.

Claudine laughed too. She came around the table and he felt

the same tap on the top of his head. This time he was fairly certain it was a kiss.

"Now you're both crazy," said Jimmy.

Later, as she served the tayglach, she looked up and said, "I am atoning for my lack of care about the world." The light outside the dining room was just beginning to wane.

"How do you mean 'lack of care,' sweetheart?" said Jimmy.

"I haven't done what I could do to ease suffering."

"Suffering where?"

"Somalia. Haiti. Baghdad. I can't even keep up with all the places anymore. People are starving, burying their children, dying under our bombs—I haven't done anything."

"Wait a minute," said Kleinman. "You have a new child."

"But I haven't done my part."

"Excuse me, what could your part be? Are you going to chain yourself to one of our airplanes?"

"It's not anything like that. You make it sound ridiculous. And you who ought to know, Grandpa Kleinman. There are things you can do: Write Congress. Inform yourself. Give to charity. *Tzedaka*—sharing of yourself. It's a venerable tradition."

"I am well aware of *tzedaka*."

"Of course you are," Claudine said. "Anyway—that is what I am atoning for this year."

Then she drank from her wine, set it down, and looked over at Jimmy.

Jimmy glanced across the table at Kleinman, then cleared his throat and said, "I guess I'm atoning for spiteful feelings at work."

"Mm-hm," Claudine said.

"You're atoning for spite at work?" said Kleinman.

"Yes. I guess so."

Kleinman drained his glass. "Spite?" he said. "When I worked, spite used to be the only thing I looked forward to. To me it was the icing on the cake."

"That's different," Jimmy said. "That was your own business. You were just enjoying the competition. I'm in a different situation."

"Well, to me it sure felt like spite."

"I think that's a perfect thing to be atoning for," said Claudine. "In Hebrew," she said, lifting her glass, "the word for 'sin' is *chayt*, which means 'missing the mark.' It's not what I grew up with, not sin the way the Catholics feel it. Missing the mark. Not doing all you could. Not being as generous as you can. And that's what spite is. I think that's lovely."

Jimmy said, "See, Pop? Not bad for a Gentile."

Then they both turned to him, and Kleinman realized grimly that he was now expected to tell them what *he* was atoning for. He took a bite of tayglach and considered what to say. The cookie was so sweet he shivered. He didn't trust any of these ceremonies. Religion was a drama staged by the fearful. Men in caves shaking clubs at the sky. Or cowering. Hank Kleinman reading Torah the day he lost his sales job at Waterbury Clock. He remembered a Thanksgiving meal with Claudine's parents, the first after she and Jimmy were married, where all the guests at the table took turns announcing what they were thankful for. When his turn had come, Kleinman looked around the fourteen places and said that what he was thankful for was that Mrs. Bishop had bought a large enough turkey.

Claudine set down her glass. "And you, Grandpa Kleinman?"

Then, from somewhere, he said, "For the hoarding of money."

"Ah," said Claudine.

"What do you mean by that, Pop?"

"It's something I've been thinking about, that's all." This surprised him.

"Do you give *tzedaka*?" asked Claudine.

"Of course I do. It's not that. I've given more than my share of that—ask anyone in Pittsburgh. That's not what I mean."

Jimmy was looking at him curiously again.

"Then what is it?" Claudine said softly.

"Nothing," Kleinman said. He'd already said more than he'd meant to. "But it was the great mistake of my days."

~~~~~~~~~~~~~~~~~~~~~~~~

A ugust was eleven years old when he and his mother arrived in America, twelve when his mother's new American boyfriend, Hank Kleinman, moved into an apartment on their floor, and thirteen when she brought out a creased envelope on a Friday evening in June and sat down across from him at the kitchen table on Beach 28th Street and Seagirt. Hank Kleinman was in shul. August was studying the Torah portion for his bar mitzvah the following week and at the same time listening to the Yankees on the radio. They were playing the Red Sox, but his mother went to the set and turned it off. "I have something important to tell you," she said. She withdrew the letter from the envelope and began to read: *"Meine sehr geehrte Frau Gertzmann,"* she began. Then she switched to English. *"I'm afraid I bear the most dreadful news."* August gulped and set down his book. *"This morning, Herr Gertzmann and Herr Gertzmann the elder"*—here his mother flinched, then switched again into German, telling him in a steady voice that his father and grandfather were dead. The letter quivered in her hands, yet he could see from her face that there was no pity in her heart at the news. This was a shock, and he was still young enough that he took most of his feelings from her; but when she reached the section of the letter, farther down the page, where the linen dyer described how the mob had been allowed into the mill, he saw her countenance harden; then abruptly it broke, and she dropped her face into her hands. In his own eyes as well, tears formed, and he came to her side of the table and reached his arms around her back. Her shoulders heaved a few times, but then she drew herself up, touched a napkin to both cheeks, and set her gaze. "This letter arrived one year ago today," she said.

August's breath caught. "And you kept it a secret?"

"Oh, Augie, what did you expect me to do?"

He looked at her. The way she had addressed him made him uncomfortable—it was as though the two of them together, somehow, were responsible for raising him.

"And next week you become a man," she said.

He rose and went to the window. "Why did we leave Hamburg?"

"Because I saw what was coming."

"What about Papa?"

"He refused to see."

"Did you try to convince him?"

"Yes."

"I don't mind it here," August said.

And the truth was he didn't. Since they had come to America, his mother's attentions had grown lighter—she was sometimes frankly joyful—and now she even had a boyfriend. Though this might have pierced August's heart, it did not, not only because of the kind of man Hank Kleinman turned out to be, but also because by then August had seen enough, in so short a time, that he was not easily discouraged. Hank Kleinman was something of a miracle, an optimistic bear of a man his mother had met on the beach at Belle Harbor. He was a religious Jew but a man of unparalleled delight. He befriended August, taught him to play stickball, which they played in yarmulkes, coached him on his grammar and his accent, chased him in the waves every Sunday, and moved into the cramped studio across from their back door a month after August's twelfth birthday, an embarrassed grin on his face as he carried his belongings up the narrow stairs that smelled of the kipper bones in the trash pail. He was a watch salesman for the Waterbury Clock Company and a dispenser of advice on every subject. He counseled August on clothing, sports, politics, history, and slang, all the while holding his mother in his huge, swooping arms. Though there were still two doors and a hallway between the apartments, in essence he was living with them.

Those were happy years, though tainted by the long shadow over them. Not from the obvious loss, for he did not miss his father or his grandfather in the least, but merely from the sense that in America only he and his mother understood the truth about the world—that Hank Kleinman could grin and take her in his arms, that he could hit August long fly balls above the lapping Atlantic waves, catch a baseball barehanded in his immense red palms, but that everywhere, beneath his mother's pealing laughter as the three of them splashed in the surf, beneath the gorgeous white beacon of her smile, was a knowledge of the world. It was just the two of them, really. Always would be, despite Hank Kleinman.

August's real father had been a tough, hard-driving man, who in his personal dealings gave the constant impression of bother. When August spoke to him in his study, he kept one hand on the page of his ledger book, running a finger down the lines of figures. When the servants addressed him at dinner, servants who had been in the household for all of August's life, he answered without looking up. And although he was refined and energetically endearing when there were guests in the house, he was invariably scornful once they had left. Something about him seethed. Hamburg then had been as fine a place as any for Jews, especially for the educated, modern ones like the Gertzmanns; but well before their flight, even August could see that things had changed. Some of the smaller Jewish stores near the Herrengraben and Bleichen canals, butcher shops and apothecaries, had been taken from their owners. There had been talk at the dinner table of the linen mill being taken as well, but Isaac Gertzmann was confident that this would never occur. The Gertzmanns were assimilated Jews, after all, listened to Haydn and Bach, no longer kept the Sabbath; they were more German than the Germans—forty of whom Isaac Gertzmann employed, he liked to say after a glass or two of port.

When later that year the Nuremberg Laws were passed, August's mother looked up from the *World-Telegram* in their kitchen on Beach 28th Street and said, "I told them this would happen." By then, of course, her husband was already two years in the grave. But August knew in his heart that she must have had all kinds of feelings to contend with; he also held the dark suspicion that the Nazis were not the only reason he and his mother had fled. There was something mean in Isaac Gertzmann, a feral bite that was not long hidden. The night of their escape, while his mother was upstairs packing, August had descended the rear staircase to locate a useful item to bring along. He chose the Peccatte and the Tourte bows—the originals, of course, but also the copies—in part because he knew they might soon need something of value, but also because he wanted to steal something that would avenge the two of them upon his father.

K leinman's company was encamped at the edge of the Aguni jungle when news reached them of Hitler's suicide, then the fall of Berlin; a week later, the surrender of the German army. But by then Kleinman felt no joy. He had been on the island for weeks now and was worn by dysentery and fear, had given up hope because, like the others, he had discovered that hope only magnified his desperation. They had secured the island and not seen evidence of a Japanese soldier in a week, but the nights were too quiet and everyone suspected a trap. He still heard weeping after lights-out. Now and then there were strange warblings from the jungle, too, which didn't sound like birds. The day the Germans surrendered in Europe, a man in his unit was whooping it up in the burned grass behind the mess tent—a tent the troops had been using for a month—when he was disemboweled by a land mine.

The jungle had been secured, but there were caves all over the island, where the enemy was hiding. The GIs went through them one by one, the most dreadful duty, rotated among the units. If the passage was wide enough, they lowered a barrel of gasoline, then exploded it with a fusillade of bullets—"ant killing," as the men called it. But some of the passages were no wider than a man's body and descended tortuously into the earth: these had to be secured by scouts. The tunnels opened onto underground rooms, where, as a soldier put his head through, the Japs might be waiting with bayonets. The enemy were smaller than the Americans and could fit through the tighter passages; as a result, the smallest of the GIs went first. Kleinman was of slight build and knew his turn would come. On watch, the lead man alternated as they moved from one cave to the next. Each squad went out once a week, and in a day they ordinarily found two or three entrances among the jumbled boulders. This meant that in general each of them took his risk only once.

Kleinman's turn came on June 4, 1945, his brother Izzy's fourth birthday. Germany had been out of the war for weeks by then, and he cursed his bitter luck to have been sent to the Pacific instead.

In the morning he wrote a letter to Ginger, then in his mind said good-bye to her; she would just then be going to sleep a half-mile from the beach he loved, twisting her hair up in pins. He wrote to his mother and stepfather, added a birthday note to his brother, and then said good-bye to them all.

That evening as his patrol came down off the high bluffs over the water, he could see the shore of the neighboring atoll, a couple of miles away, which was still held by the Japanese. Now and then signal flares went up, but there was no fire coming in from the ships and the night was silent. Below them, between the impenetrable jungle canopy in which they walked and the short beach that gave onto the waterways between the reefs, lay a steep descent of rubble and limestone; in among the rocks were the caves. They'd scouted two empty dead-ends that afternoon and it was now Kleinman's turn to lead. In the remaining light, the patrol spread itself out among the cascading shale. Kleinman himself was the one who found the entrance, a set of small boulders that had been improbably stacked one upon the other; he tilted the top one aside and an opening appeared.

Of course he could have simply walked on. But along with the fear that had settled inside him on this island had come an equally dreadful sense of fate—the feeling that this was *his* cave, that to skip it would mean more certain doom than the chance he would take crawling through. If he skipped it, he would have to enter the next one down the line, the one found by the grinning, terrified Baptist boy up ahead of him or the silent, mournful Swede from North Dakota, whom Kleinman could see poking halfheartedly with his rifle butt near the waterline.

The unit took up positions for his entrance, and in the last light of evening—it was almost nine o'clock and the sun was finally gone—Kleinman pulled back the two sheltering boulders and stepped aside for reconnaissance: sloping to the east out of sight ran a passage no wider than his shoulders. He stood back: a grenade was useless and would alert the enemy. He pulled off his helmet, then slung his rifle tight against his shoulder with the bayonet forward, inserted his small flashlight into his mouth, and moved to his hands and knees. He made the first turn into the blackness, thinking of Ginger in her bed; but then the passageway narrowed, fear engulfed him, and he extended his arms forward and moved down flat onto the ground. Water trickled beneath, soaking him. The stone roof and walls pressed close. With his hands ahead, he was able to feel the turns of the tunnel before he descended into them, but soon it was sloping so steeply down that he feared he might plummet if it widened. He pushed onward for what he judged to be ten feet, the passageway narrowing until he had to wedge one shoulder through ahead of the other, propelling himself with pushes of his toes. Then it leveled somewhat and he paused and looked for light in the distance: pure dark, not even his own arms visible in front of him; the sound in his ears of trickling water. On his face the slight movement of cool air: this meant a second entrance. It also meant a cave the enemy was likely to choose. He began to weep in silence, unable to move his hands to his face; they came up of their own accord, and his bayonet tapped against the rock. The enemy could be waiting for him an inch beyond his fingers. Blackness in front of him. Doom. If he didn't come out in an hour, the unit would return with reinforcements. He thought again of Ginger. He closed his eyes and sent his thoughts to her: *I love you, my angel—I am thinking of you always.* Then he vowed that if he ever made it home, he would marry her, live a quiet life, and bring children into the world.

The ringing of the running stream water was louder in his ears and now from the distance came the hollow sound of droplets: a pool perhaps, or a cavern. He exhaled deeply and wedged himself through the narrow closure. He was able to wriggle forward, first shoulders, then chest, then hips. The tunnel turned, widening, and now he convinced himself that he was traveling upward, arcing back toward the plateau, where the roots of the great trees and the strangling vines found their way downward through gaps in the rock; the passageway was wide enough that he could bend his knees slightly and propel his weight forward.

On the troopship later, after Nagasaki and the enemy surrender, he would wonder why he hadn't simply waited out his turn in the cave and then crawled back out. Nobody in his unit would have known whether he'd found anything. But at the time, his fingers exploring the widening gap before him, he hadn't even considered turning back. The other men were relying on him. This was the fundamental trick of the military, he would realize on deck that morning: the honor of camaraderie. But at the time, in the cave, some other sense had simply entered him. Perhaps it was courage: despite the fear that made him weep again, as quietly as he could, still unable to move his hands to his face, he knew he would continue farther. With his arms he felt inside the narrow rim of the passage, then arched himself through.

The channel grew level, then widened. He reached up—room

enough to crawl now, and, after a few more feet, to stand: a cavern. From the far end came the splash of a waterfall. He stood, moved his Garand into his hands, felt for the safety, and released it. He was prepared to die now, prepared for the blow of a bayonet in the blackness. He crouched, straining his eyes for the glint of metal. He pulled the flashlight from his mouth and held it in front of him, his hand on the switch. *I love you Ginger; I am thinking of you always.* He flashed it on and then off: a hallway of sorts. At the end, black. He reached to the wall for his bearings, then passed through.

The moisture was cool now on his face and the water rushed in earnest: he was inside the lip of a hollow. He stood still, flattened against the wall, straining into the dark. Then, underneath the roar of the waterfall, he heard an animal snorting: a wild boar. He was in its den! He'd once seen a herd of them stampeding at the edge of the palms, their tusks in the air, after the grinning Baptist boy, crazed with homesickness, had lost his cool and shot one on the beach. The boy had wanted to roast it and had begun to bawl when instead the C.O. had kicked the carcass into the sea. Now the animal seemed to be off to his left and some distance away, perhaps on the other side of the cavern. Kleinman stood unmoving, his rifle pointed low to ward off a charge. The sound came no closer, and he realized there might be a lake between them. With his feet he felt for the topography of the floor, in case he would have to move for cover, then lowered himself again to a squat. He held the flashlight switch, his hand shaking, listening for the snorts and trying to discern the direction from which they came. The sound was confusing, mixed with the waterfall. He heard it low and to his left, nine o'clock and at the level of the floor. *I love you Ginger, I am thinking of you always.* He flipped the flashlight on and off: ten feet in front of him lay a sleeping Japanese soldier.

~~~~~~~~~~~~~~~~~~~~~~~~~~~~~~

F or a period he became interested in painting—not because it was an investment, but because one afternoon in 1972 at a fund-raiser in the home of a wealthy benefactor of the Carnegie Museum of Art, Kleinman paused before a solitary oil by Francis Bacon and was swept up and into it. The crowd around him was mixed, the genteel descendants of Carnegie himself and of the other titans of the era—a woman named Rocky Hines, whose first name, apparently, was Rockefeller, a talkative man named Cornelius Vanderbilt Whitney, who wore a folded purple handkerchief in the breast pocket of his jacket—but also the pork-packing and bauxite-mining and cement-milling men, whose histories Kleinman knew upon first sight, men imbued with the wariness and pugnacious self-surprise of a generation that had made its own wealth. Kleinman in truth felt equally interested in both sets. In the Vanderbilts and Mellons, because they seemed most certainly doomed to him, dissipated by the very wealth he had worked all his life to attain—this frightened him for his own children—and by the pork and cement and bauxite men, because he was combative and could not keep himself from making comparisons. Upon meeting, these men sniffed out one another like dogs. A rival's actual wealth they intended to discern during the first five minutes of conversation. A few never went beyond that, but most of them, satisfied finally that Kleinman was running a different race—the beer-brewing race and not the auto-supply or soap-milling or garbage-collection race—dropped the wariness and admitted a chuckle to be standing in such a crowd, amid the Carnegies in their Christmas jackets of red and green, the Rodin sculptures cut in ice amid the platters of oysters, and the restored Etruscan mosaic across the vast ceiling, given faux support by columns of pink Italian marble.

It was alongside one of these columns that Kleinman found the Francis Bacon, alone on a small, shaded wall. It was a morbid scene, a carcass of beef tethered to a hook among shadows of dark and further dark. Here and there the shining red of blood. Yet he was transfixed by the artistry of the effect. He stepped close and attempted to understand the placement of the brushstrokes—the small thrusts of crimson emerging from the darkness as though illuminated from within. The beauty of the color and yet its intrinsic insistence on brutality. He had never before been interested in painting. The very subjects—landscapes, royalty—eluded him. And now this single scene.

He inquired of one of the guides, a straight-backed young art student from Carnegie-Mellon who stood fidgeting in the corner. The painter, she told him, was an Irish-born Englishman, a rogue and dissipant, a horse trainer's son and a notorious eccentric who became a self-taught master in oils.

Kleinman said, "Where can I buy one?"

Later, he was embarrassed to have asked such a question. But it was understandable among such a crowd that the young woman did not even smile. "Christie's, I would think," she said seriously, and, when he looked puzzled, added, "In London."

That spring, without telling Ginger, he sent over an expert, who returned with what he wanted—two recent Bacons and, of the man's own choosing, a dark still-life by Morandi. Kleinman was referred to a craftsman in Youngstown who made frames for them of box-jointed mahogany. The frames were exquisite, nearly as appealing to Kleinman as the paintings themselves, and their maker, who delivered the items in person, turned out to be a Japanese about the age of one of Kleinman's sons. Kleinman had never had a Japanese in his house, but he found in the first few moments after opening the door that he bore no ill feeling for the race. The framer was twenty years too young to have been in the war. He was slender of build but possessed a carver's strong forearms, and he impressed Kleinman deeply with his courtly air and the muscular precision of his hands. His fingers moved over the frames, picking at bits of dust. He was also a calligrapher, Kleinman discovered.

Without intending to, Kleinman said, "I have another type of work for you, if you're interested."

"What is it?"

"A translation."

He went down to the basement, where in his old government-issue trunk he found the burlap bag and untied it. Its contents were undamaged by time, the palette of stiffened leather, the stylus on a chain, the neatly tied bundle of nearly translucent rice paper covered in an excruciating and beautiful Japanese hand. The darkness of the trunk had perfectly preserved the ink. He brought the palette upstairs and asked for a translation and a set of frames in which to display it.

⌇⌇⌇⌇⌇⌇⌇⌇⌇⌇⌇⌇⌇⌇⌇⌇⌇

The week of his sixty-fifth birthday, Ginger signed them up for a class in CPR at the Jewish Community Center in Squirrel Hill. The idea was morbid, though of course Kleinman could also see her reasoning. But he didn't like the way she'd been acting lately—too solicitous of him; when she held his elbow now in winter he had a sense that it was his own balance, not hers, that she was worried about. Why? Because one day, while fixing a tile that had come loose on the roof, he had become dizzy and had to come down off the ladder. The doctor had examined him and found nothing wrong but his cholesterol. He had to change his diet, walk more, take two pills, and everything would be okay. Yet this small news made its way into everything Ginger did. Certain expressions. Certain movements of the hands, the ushering gestures used with a child. The turning at every cough. It chafed at him.

In CPR class they practiced on flesh-colored dummies that emitted the smell of alcohol and plastic. At one point they had to practice the sharp blow to the sternum, and he watched the tears form, then well, in his wife's downturned eyes as she leaned over the reclining model and struck it with her tiny balled-up hand. He pictured himself as he might look to her from above, splayed on a snowy sidewalk. She let her fist rest on the mannequin's breastbone where she had struck it, then pulled it back and struck again, and the tears spilled onto her cheeks. He turned away.

~~~~~~~~~~~~~~~~~~~~~~~~~~~~~~~

In August the war ended in the Pacific and he found himself on a ship again, bound once more for San Francisco, an intoxicating lightness now inside him. He stood at the rails watching the sea churn past, aware for the second time in his life of the grace that seemed to flirt at the edge of his days. No Japanese torpedoes lurked beneath the slate-colored sea, which peaked, rolled, and then slid away behind the sharp-cut stern as though saluting the decked soldiers in a tumble of joy. There was meat on board now, and smuggled whiskey. The men gambled recklessly at cards, showed pictures around, stood arm-over-shoulder in rows of tens with their comrades at the gently bobbing prow. In San Francisco they left ship at Fort MacDowell, on Angel Island, and more than a few of the soldiers walked to where the eucalyptus trees rose alongside the paved jetties and kissed the crumbly, black earth. From San Francisco he found himself on a night-hop aboard a C-69 Constellation, back to New York. A week after that, early on a crisp Saturday morning in September 1945, he was discharged from Fort Dix, New Jersey, and boarded the train to Penn Station. Two hours later, in Wavecrest, he sprinted up the stairs to the walk-up and greeted his mother in her robe. Hank Kleinman came out to the hall a moment later, and it was he, his old stepfather in a tallith, who burst into tears. His own mother, Kleinman realized with a flicker of melancholy, had learned to ward off both pain and, in consequence, such ecstasies as Hank Kleinman now shared with him. This was the world.

They hugged and went inside, and Kleinman told them the stories of his tour in the Pacific, while Izzy, grown to be a spindly four-year-old in the time away, brought out his battle drawings and pushed in next to him on the dinette. August took him in his lap. Hank Kleinman kept reaching across the table and ruffling both their heads with his huge hands. Then suddenly, as though a dam had come down, his mother began weeping in earnest. He was a bona fide hero to them, he saw now, but it was not for anything he'd done in the East China Sea; it was simply for the fact that he'd returned. This was his parents' view, he finally understood as he watched Hank Kleinman grimace during the tale of his days on Aguni-jima. Of his ordeal in the cave he said nothing, for the tale of his fright seemed both too vivid and too bitter to reveal. They wouldn't care about what he'd done, that he'd risked his life for the Allied forces. Hank Kleinman was a pacifist by nature—an old-world Jew, the kind who would have gone easily to the camps—and to him the only victory possible was this: a son (for this was how he now thought of August) back at the kitchen table, drinking Pepsi Cola. August was disappointed—how could he not be? But only for a moment. Then the logic of it struck him as well, that his parents were absolutely right. The disappointment, as once had his fear, turned to anger. And later, when his politics changed, this was the moment to which he returned—the kitchen table, the salt scent of the air in Rockaway, Hank Kleinman's familiar hand on his head. He had been picked up like sand in the cyclone of the times but then, miraculously, set back down. There was no more to it than that. The war was over and he had lived.

In the evening he walked over to see Ginger. She could not have understood the feelings that stirred inside him when her mother, having hurried from the kitchen to greet him, retreated to the back of the apartment through a door that closed, then opened again in a moment to reveal Ginger herself, a backward gearing of time, in a pale green camisole and with her hair pulled up in a bun. The heat of the ardor he felt at that moment was specifically proportional, he understood, to the terror he had known— to the actual moments of crawling through the lair of the enemy, as though the depth of that horror and hatred now translated into a deeper room inside himself—and into that room, as he watched Ginger push aside the pillows on the settee and arrange herself, entered a profound and unbreakable tenderness.

The moment they returned to the apartment after their walk, not two hours later, the sky still light at that time in summer and the air smelling of the evening's cooking, her mother came forward from the kitchen to greet them, her hands out to grasp his this time, as though she already knew what they had found in each other. And perhaps she did. Perhaps his face, perhaps her daughter's too, had been as transparent as her own—a smile of relief and woe together, a woman come out in her apron, away from the steaming stove, to give away her most precious possession in the world.

That was what the war did for him. It made him sure of what he wanted. And in return others acknowledged him as well. This was no small gift.

~~~~~~

Pop, you're absolutely positive you don't want to come?" Jimmy asked. "It's Kol Nidre."

"I could ask the same of you," said Kleinman.

"We go every year. We like it."

Kleinman could see that Jimmy and Claudine were taking their time preparing for services. "Well," he said. "For my own part, I could not be more dead-set."

"And you're sure you'll be okay with him?"

"You never asked when it was you I was taking care of."

"I never had the chance," Jimmy said.

Kleinman enjoyed this kind of talk. It was like eating. But in his son's voice there was always a recognizable glimmer of petulance that put the repartee, somehow, on more dangerous ground. He decided not to answer him.

"Come on, Pop—let me show you how to do everything."

"You don't think I've done it all a thousand times? The world might have changed, Jimmy, but thank God nothing's changed about babies."

"Pop, you know Mom did it all. Come on, I'll show you."

In the nursery, Kleinman glanced around. "Everything's changed," he said. The room had a green glow to it from some kind of electronic night-light. Kleinman stared at it: the size of a credit card. It gave off a radiance, a vision of the future.

Jimmy said, "I'll do this one. You watch. You do the next one."

"How does that light work? Where's the bulb?"

"Watch, Pop. We're late. You'll have to do the next one."

"I changed ten thousand diapers when you were in such a crib."

"You did not."

"You're right, your mother did it all, didn't she? God bless her."

"The diapers are paper now."

"I know that. Do I look like I've been living in Abyssinia?"

"Here, look. You rest him on the pad. Then you strap him in so he doesn't roll off. We'll be gone two hours. And we'll call you as soon as we get to temple. And then again at nine. When the phone rings at nine, you can pick it up. It will be us."

Kleinman said, "We never used a strap."

"Well, we do now."

"We never had a velvet bed like this, either."

"It's not a velvet bed, Pop. It's a changing table."

"Do you know where we changed you?"

"Now, watch—first you strap him in. Then you put the new diaper under, in case he goes while you're changing him, then you pull off the old one. See?"

"We changed you on top of the refrigerator. It was an old Philco, the low model with a flat top. That's where we changed you. We didn't use a strap."

"Well, now we do it like this. And I have my pager, too, remember. It's set to vibration. The number is on the fridge. You can always page me. And don't forget to strap him in. Look how I do it. First the new one. Under. Pull. Close. The Velcro tabs are great. You can reposition them. Look at these things. On second thought, we'll use the signal when we call. One ring, then hang up. Then we'll call back. I'll call you at nine."

"Velcro—" Kleinman said.

"Are you listening?"

"I wish I had thought of Velcro. In 1956 Maurie Sharf sat down at our kitchen table with an idea of his. You know what it was?"

"Pop, watch me."

"It was bubble wrap. Did I give him money? No, I laughed at him."

"Pop, watch. You might have to change him."

"But I did all right anyway."

"Pull the tabs tight," Jimmy said. "So they don't leak. The old one goes in here." He reached the diaper over a circular contraption, opened the lid, and twisted.

"What the hell is that?"

"Gets rid of the smell." He twisted again and closed the lid. "You don't smell anything in here, do you?"

"How am I ever going to learn what you just did?"

"You don't have to. It's only services, and we won't stay the whole time. We're going to be out for two hours at most. And I'll call to check in when we get there. Mrs. Diamond next door knows what's happening. She's got five kids. And I'll call in an hour, too. Listen for the signal. Just leave the dirties on the table."

"How much did that machine cost you?"

"Which machine?"

"The diaper thing. The one for the smells."

"A gift. Why?"

"And those diapers with the Velcro. They're top-of-the-line, aren't they?"

"They're good diapers, yes. They keep him dry. Otherwise he gets a rash."

"I think your lovely wife likes to spend your money—"

From the kitchen came a loud laugh.

"What's that about?" Kleinman said.

"Claudine happens to be very frugal."

Another laugh.

"Is she crazy in there or what?"

"The baby monitor," Jimmy answered, pointing to a little white box like a radio. "The baby monitor's on."

A ugust knew little English when he arrived in America, and he was kept back a year in school. But soon, with Hank Kleinman's coaching, he began to shed his accent, and by the eighth grade he had begun to forget his German. He was a rapid learner but only an average student at P.S. 106 and then Far Rockaway High School, where he sat between a boy named Klein and another named Kleinzhaler, both of whom, he later discovered, became doctors. Despite his intelligence and the relative quiet of his demeanor, bookishness was not in his nature. He was always flirting with misbehavior. At Far Rockaway High his thoughts ran to stickball, the war, which had recently started in Europe, the Dodgers at Ebbets Field, the amusement park at Coney Island, and now and then the punishing fistfight that the Irish bully in their class, Ned Hagney, dealt out after school with a pale, sneering face. Secretly, August hoped he would be singled out for a match. He wouldn't have minded letting loose a few blows, even if it meant a whipping. But perhaps Ned Hagney could see this, too, for as he went through the class, he skipped over August and settled one by one on the boys who, as everyone could see, most feared it. This was fine in the end with Kleinman, and certainly taught him a lesson. A feeling of bravado was waking inside him. Maybe it was his past. In school he walked with his shoulders slightly raised.

But it was also his mother's dictum taking hold. *Take the advice of no one.* That was what school was for him, really—long sessions of advice. Trigonometry, where even before Pearl Harbor they had been learning to calculate bomb trajectories. Grammar, at which he excelled despite being a latecomer to the language. History, which droned in his ears. Civics, which puzzled him. He was wary of it all. Even in English class, where Mr. DeLeo singled him out as an exemplar, called him to the board to parse outrageous sentences from the Gettysburg Address and the novels of William Faulkner, he took part only warily. Even then he was resistant to acting someone else's part. Who, after all, could be trusted? It was in his blood.

In the summer of 1940, his mother and Hank Kleinman were married by a judge, and in June 1941 his brother, Izzy, was born. Kleinman was nineteen and, despite being the stepchild, found himself overwhelmed with feeling for the tiny, wrinkled mass in the front-room bassinet. Izzy was born with a mild case of jaundice and never took well to the bottle—he was a tiny newborn and remained a very tiny baby. This produced sympathy in everyone, but it was more than that: August somehow felt as though he himself were in part the father, the protector of the family. It even occurred to him that he might someday want children of his own. That winter, his mother's new husband had legally adopted him; and shortly afterward, at his mother's suggestion, August had gone to City Hall to change his name from Gertzmann to Kleinman. On the train ride home, he practiced his new role in the world. "Good to meet you," he said into the cold, clouding window of the crowded passenger car. "August Kleinman's the name."

"W hat's this?" Kleinman asked.

"That's Claudine's pump."

"Her pump?"

"Her breast pump."

"Yes," Kleinman said. "I hear about them at Bread and Circus." He probably seemed like a demented old man to Jimmy. Women talked about breast pumps quite a bit, in fact. Kleinman had actually heard entire conversations on the subject. Young mothers waiting at the checkout, their infants in the wagons. Jimmy stepped into the hall and Kleinman went over to examine the thing. It sat in a black leather bag, a large purse with a shoulder strap. Inside he could see various funnels, plastic cups, and tubing. When Jimmy and Harry and Hannah were young, Ginger never went to work. Never needed such a device. But it didn't look bad. He lifted the flap and examined the design. Perhaps it was better that mothers worked; it was a change that his generation lamented in their daughters, but to Kleinman's mind work was a tonic. Getting out of the house was a tonic. Just that act alone—walking in a clean shirt, with damp hair, as the sun rose over the world. Why shouldn't a lady want that, too?

"Haven't you ever seen one?" Jimmy said.

Kleinman pulled back his hands.

"She uses it when she has to go out."

"I think it's good," he said.

"What's good?"

"That Claudine gets out. It's good for her. Good for Asher, too, for that reason. Even if he misses her a few minutes. That way he learns to trust himself."

"I didn't know you'd been thinking about it, Pop."

~~~~~~~~~~~~~~~~~~~~~~~~~~~~~

Ginger agreed to marry him. In the fall of 1945 they traveled to Boston, where her people lived, North End Italians either uncharacteristically liberal or who had been instructed to treat him well. He was not quite twenty-four. Her uncle owned a restaurant and fed the two of them while dozens of relatives filed in to greet them. Kleinman made a point of ordering sausage, and the uncle made a point of asking him whether he knew what it contained. It was remarkably easy, such a peccadillo, after returning from the Pacific. And delicious, too. After lunch they took the streetcar to the Back Bay and Ginger showed him around, making a plea, he later realized, for them to settle in Boston. That too was why her relatives, whom he had expected to shun him, had fed him huge plates of food instead; there had been only two men born into the family in a generation, it turned out, and the only other marriage among the sisters was to a meat-packer, who'd taken his bride back to Chicago. There were restaurants and a drapery-cleaning business: Kleinman was being offered an income.

But he turned it down. *Take the advice of no one.* They spent three days in Boston and Ginger made a run of it, taking him to the little candy stores and dress shops she remembered from her childhood and to the sights Kleinman himself knew from his history books, their promise of someone else's country—Paul Revere's house, Harvard Square, the burial ground at Copp's Hill. But on the fourth day he cut the visit short and brought her back down with him to New York. On the train they argued in low voices and he saw for the first time the surprising tenacity that in later years would become his own strength and counsel; yet he prevailed by telling her he needed to make his own way in the world. This seemed to convince her. In turn, she wanted an adventure and preferred not to stay in New York. He compromised on that point, and together, from a dime-store atlas, they chose Pittsburgh, Pennsylvania, where two great rivers converged, a city that a man on his ship had once told him was on the cusp of a boom.

They were married that winter, and then for two years in Pittsburgh he was a luggage salesman for Portland Suitcase, a job that acquainted him with all the department stores north of Baltimore and south of Newark, New Jersey. Portland Suitcase produced a leather valise and a Pullman, and a new line in doctors' bags with accordion louvers at the aperture. He called on department stores and surgical suppliers and was making a reasonable living; these were the postwar times—train and ocean-liner travel were booming; Pan American Airlines could fly a man around the world. On visits home now, he talked all manner of sales with Hank Kleinman.

He and Ginger rented a one-bedroom apartment overlooking the Monongahela, with cork floors and slatted windows and a public park in back, where they sat on a wrought-iron bench in the evenings and watched the bluebirds. She was a natural gardener, it turned out, an attribute he had never known in anyone. In Wavecrest, his mother's plants had always died in their pots, reduced to twiggy stems that she replaced each spring from diggings taken from behind the boardwalk. Now, at the rear of the Pittsburgh apartment's sunny grounds, Ginger hoed a plot and put in vegetables and flowers behind a squirrel fence, beds and beds of variegated tulips that sprang to life every spring, a cage full of tropical birds. She wrote away to a relative in Europe and received in the mail a thick brown envelope full of bulbs and seeds. Every evening when he returned, he set down his briefcase and walked to the back of the apartment, where through the slatted windows he watched her in the raised beds, bent on her knees, producing by magic and will this strange abundance. With his wife he was happy, but in his work he was not.

When he mentioned this to Hank Kleinman, he received warnings and admonitions. Yet as he drove the long hours between Pittsburgh and his customers in Washington and Baltimore and Philadelphia, he thought incessantly of what he might do instead. He wanted to make something. He considered starting his own luggage concern. He considered a candy factory—there was a German company interested in expanding into the United States with its *pfefferminze* candy—PEZ, it was called; he considered Automats, an idea presented to him by a salesman he met at a lunch counter in Harrisburg. But nothing struck him with finality until one afternoon, standing near the Ohio with Ginger, all the water flowing past him suddenly gave him the idea that transformed his life.

The framer arrived with the first installment, two different sets of pages displayed elegantly in double rice-colored mats, hung again in box-jointed African mahogany, the new calligraphy equally elegant in English. He bowed in Kleinman's entrance hall and then bowed again when he set the frames on his dining room table. Kleinman had asked him to read the journal and to translate whatever caught his attention. He did not know what to expect. He was worried that he had chosen a Japanese to do the work—

but what choice did he have? He suddenly feared that the writing would turn out to be thirty-year-old military secrets, that he had breached his loyalty to the U.S. Army. This he felt even after all the intervening years and the sea change in his feelings: the depth of his alarm startled him. But he saw immediately that he was wrong. One of the letters seemed to be nothing more than a description of the soldier's idle daydreams; it began:

> *I miss as much as anything else the face of the mountain at dawn,*
> *when it clothes itself, shyly, in the waters of Lake Ashi.*

The other, less densely covered in script, seemed to be bits of poetry. Haiku, perhaps—Kleinman didn't know the form. Here, the framer had doubled the display, placing the original Japanese above the calligraphed translation. He read aloud: *"Araumiya— Sado ni yokotau—Amanogawa."* Then, in an accent that sounded only like eastern Ohio, he went on, pointing to the translation:

> *The rough sea—*
> *extending toward Sado Isle,*
> *The Milky Way*

He bowed again, and Kleinman, profoundly satisfied with the pieces, brought them to the mantel, where he leaned them against the plaster, stepped back from the wall, and bowed in return, hesitantly. When he rose, he saw immediately that they were the most beautiful items in the room, more beautiful than the Morandi even, in their lustrous frames. He offered the man a cup of tea, and it was at this point that the framer pulled out the last of the packages from his portfolio. This one was more carefully wrapped than the others, sealed in twine rather than tape, and it took him several moments to remove the rice paper. He cut the knots with a nail clipper, refolded the wrapping, and wound the twine onto a wooden peg. To Kleinman, this was a pleasing meticulousness as well.

"This one, I believe, is a letter to his beloved . . ." The framer raised it to the mantel.

> *March 19th, 1945 (Monday? Sunday?)*
> *Aguni-jima, East China Sea*

My Most Divine Umi—
 You cannot imagine how I long for you.

At nine, the door opened. "What happened to the signal?" Kleinman said.

"We decided we'd rather be with you and Asher," said Claudine. She went straight into the nursery.

"You decided an hour of dogma was too much."

"No," Jimmy said.

"You decided you didn't think Grandpa Augie could take care of a baby."

"No."

Claudine came back out. "He's asleep."

"Of course he's asleep," said Kleinman.

"How was he?"

"Perfect. An angel. I liked him. He liked me. We were partners."

"Did he wake up?"

"No."

"Did you have to change him?"

"No."

"What did you do?"

"Read the paper. First Yom Kipper in ten years I wasn't at a movie."

Claudine disappeared into the kitchen. "There's something I forgot," she called out to the living room. Then she emerged carrying a candle. "*Yahrzeit,*" she said. "I forgot to do it at dinner."

"Translation?" said Jimmy.

Kleinman said, "You need your wife to tell you this?"

"It's a ritual, isn't it?" Jimmy said. "Claudine knows all of them. What's this one, honey?"

Kleinman said, "Quiet—" It had been forty years since he'd said a prayer aloud with his stepfather, but now he joined his daughter-in-law: "... *asher kidshanu b'mitzvotav vitzivanu l'hadlik ner shel Yom HaKippurim.*"

"What was that anyway?" Jimmy said when they had finished. He had picked up the sports page. Then, "What's the matter, Pop?"

"It's a memorial," said Claudine. "To your mother."

"Oh, Pop," Jimmy said, rising from the sofa. "I'm sorry, I didn't know. I didn't realize—"

～～～～～～～～～～～～～～～～～～～

G inger never completed her degree, but sometimes, after the children were grown, she spoke of the possibility of returning to college. It usually came up during their walks, which they took every morning now, Ginger wearing a sweat suit in the cold months, swinging a pair of dark blue dumbbells in her hands. This was the 1980s and she was past sixty already, a fact surprising enough to wake Kleinman now and then in bed, where he turned and regarded her next to him. How was it possible that she looked nearly the same to him as when they were married? For years now she had read every issue of *Scientific American*—as absurd to him as if it were an excerpt of the Koran arriving monthly in their mailbox, wrapped in thin brown paper, for her to amuse herself with over tea. At Pennsylvania College for Women, before Harry was born, she had talked about becoming a chemist. But Kleinman had not really paid attention to those words then—his mind was occupied every moment by the future; yet now, halfway around the great orbit of their lives, here he was, hearing them again. She always brought it up at the end of their exercise, her tongue loosened by the exertion

Kleinman, for his part, walked in a plain black overcoat, his hands in the pockets. Cold weather stiffened his joints. And these days he got all the exercise he needed worrying about the breweries, which lately had come under the gaze of a couple of tough-talking young lawyers from one of the behemoth Midwestern food corporations. The big boys were muscling around in his territory. In truth, he might have considered letting go if the right offer were made, but he didn't like that they sent such young men to see him. In his office he sat back in his reclining leather chair and listened as first they made their tenders in terms only an attorney would understand; then, when he remained unconvinced, switched without interruption to a series of rather vulgar threats. It brought back memories. But this time he was unmoved, either to fear or to anger. He offered Glenfiddich around, which they mistakenly took as assent, then showed them the door. By himself, he went for a walk along the river.

The thought passed before him that he could get out. Retire. Hannah had gone off to Bucknell; the boys were on their own; Ginger was speaking of a return to school. Why shouldn't he, too, throw the ballast overboard and set off toward another horizon? When he asked Ginger what she thought he might do in retirement, she said, "Give away your money."

"What?"

"Give it away." They stood at a corner, waiting for the traffic light. She pumped the dumbbells in her hands. "You've made it. Now give it back. Start a foundation."

"What? That's for Carnegies. Not Kleinmans."

And that was all they spoke of it. Looking back now, he realized that the conversation was probably what kept him in business another decade, the quick guillotine of fear he had felt at the suggestion. In the fifties, the College for Women had changed its name to Chatham College; in the summer of 1988, he sent them a donation, and that fall Ginger enrolled again, more than forty years after she'd left, to finish a degree in chemistry. When Kleinman pulled the Lincoln up to the lab building on winter evenings, there she was again through the tall, warped windows, swirling an Erlenmeyer flask over the blue-yellow comet of a Bunsen flame. He liked to go inside, stand next to her at the burn-scarred linoleum bench while she worked studiously beside him. Around them, the other students milled about like children. Ginger didn't like to talk while she worked. If he spoke to her, she answered with a frost of reprimand in her voice. It still thrilled him.

Jimmy and Claudine were in Boston, visiting Kleinman in his new condominium. They took a car ride to see a regatta on the Charles, were driving by Mass General, when suddenly Jimmy turned into the lot. "What's happened?" said Kleinman.

"We're seeing a doctor for you. A cardiologist."

"No we're not."

"Yes we are."

"No dice. Turn the car around."

"It's a done deal. We're here."

"Are you crazy? This is no Podunk hospital. You can't just drive in and expect to see anyone."

"We have an appointment," Claudine said from the backseat. "You're seeing Jerome Wolff. The very best in the world. He's the heart man for all the heads of state. He was Menachem Begin's doctor."

"And that's supposed to recommend him?"

"And Elie Wiesel's," said Claudine.

"He sounds like a geriatric case."

"Pop, you need to see someone."

"I don't need to do anything."

"It's not for you," Claudine said. "It's for us."

Dr. Wolff's office looked out over the river. The regatta was about to begin: Kleinman watched the sailboats gather together behind the bridge, sheep crowding a pen. Before he even saw the doctor he was given an EKG and a checkup by a nurse. Kleinman didn't like being treated like an animal. He was ready for this Dr. Wolff. But as it turned out, he liked him right away. Something of the man's name in the face. A lupine expression, though tired—he appeared simultaneously amused and hard-nosed. A Jew who could appear to be a Gentile if he wanted but could also be a Jew. Kleinman had always liked that: a trait of the successful. Bifocals and an expensive set of clothing.

Dr. Wolff asked him some questions, listened with the stethoscope, then recommended a treadmill test.

Kleinman said, "Treadmills are for mules."

"And are we all not mules?" said Wolff. He smiled wryly as he set his stethoscope back into his pocket. "I'm only interested to see if the pain is indeed cardiac in origin."

"It's not pain."

"The feeling. The discomfort."

"What if I don't want to know?"

"A good question," Wolff said. "What if I told you it can be treated?"

"With what? An operation? No operations for me."

"Often, medically. With medicines. No operation."

"It's heartache," Kleinman said. "I know what it is."

"This is only to make sure of that, Mr. Kleinman."

"Dr. Wolff, do you have a wife?"

"Passed away," the doctor said. "Married over thirty years."

"Fifty for me," Kleinman said. "Then you understand."

"Yes, I do," the doctor answered. He removed his bifocals and steamed them with his breath, then rubbed them on the cuff of his shirt. Kleinman recognized that he had wounded him.

"All right, Doc," he said. "Give me the test."

He went on the treadmill that afternoon, in a room in the hospital where a young lady in a rather short skirt observed him. It turned out she was a cardiologist as well. Kleinman ran harder for her—he couldn't help himself. Then she told him to stop. He couldn't talk for a moment. She was silent as well, writing on a pad.

Kleinman became worried. "Well," he finally said. "Is it the ticker?"

"There's a touch of ST depression laterally," she answered.

"What is that supposed to mean?"

"Yes, it's your heart."

"No surgery," Kleinman said. "I told him that."

"Dr. Wolff will want to do a cath."

"What's that?"

"Another test."

So he had the catheterization, two weeks later. It necessitated another plane flight for Jimmy and Claudine. The needle was inserted near his groin, which needless to say he found rather barbaric, and afterward he was required to lie with a sandbag over his hip. This time the results were good. Or so said Dr. Wolff. A blockage in an artery, but still only a single one. Kleinman considered it bad news, but the doctor seemed not to. There would be no surgery. Three prescriptions, however; Claudine wheeled him downstairs to fill them.

The pills came in brown pharmaceutical bottles, names he couldn't keep straight in his head. "The beginning of the end," he said.

"God in heaven," answered Claudine. "Don't be maudlin."

Kleinman liked that.

~~~~~~~~~~~~~~~~~~~~~~~~~~~~~~~~

A fter he had grown wealthy, after he owned three breweries and employed seventy-five men, after the downtown bankers had begun sending him Christmas cards, he remembered the moment the idea had come to him and marveled at his own hubris in taking it up: the chances must have been a thousand to one. He had his savings and the small amount that an uncle of Ginger's had left to them, and with it he enticed Sherman Gerstein, of the Gerst's Department Store family, to come into business with him. This was 1948. He'd known Sherman Gerstein from his sales calls with Portland Suitcase, and the man agreed to join up as a silent partner.

Through the Gerstein family's connections, Kleinman hired a brewmaster named Christoph Cerny, from a village outside of Pilsen, Czechoslovakia, who had been running a lunch counter in Allentown; twenty miles upstream from the Pittsburgh furnaces, he leased a warehouse on the Allegheny, and from a firm in Wisconsin he bought a single copper vat, which came floating up to the back windows on an ore barge one cold, rainy morning in April. Truman was in the White House. The country was booming: Kaiser-Frazer automobiles; Jack Benny and Fred Allen; Ella Fitzgerald and Duke Ellington. Ginger had spent two years in college before she gave birth to Harry, who was old enough now to walk. An athletic toddler, seemingly without fear. This somehow inspired Kleinman. It was now or never, he realized. He had resigned the luggage job and moved a chair and a desk into the warehouse, which stood on a bluff from which he could look out over the river at the giant Alcoa smelters downstream in New Kensington and at the low-laden barges moving stealthily among the locks. In front of his window the water ran clear, straight down out of the Allegheny Mountains, not yet turned green-brown by the discharge pumps at the furnaces and foundries; it ran sparkling and twinkling underneath the loading pier on which, a month later, lay his first shipment of malt, hops, and cereal.

He was frightened. Yet downriver he could see the fierce furnaces throwing blue-black smoke into the air, the crude ore of the land being transformed by human ingenuity into girders and beams that were then floated downstream to ports and train yards and trucking depots, a vast delta of commerce that fanned out from there to all the great hubs of the earth. The sight braced him.

And Pittsburgh, as he watched, was being rebuilt. This was the beginning of its renaissance: great towers rising, the ash-filled air cleaned, parks and fountains set grandly into the landscape. The marvel of human endeavor and recompense. Christoph Cerny had worked in breweries all through Europe, and with the Gerstein family's credit they were able to purchase the draining ducts and gas burners and the steel fermenting chamber into which the wort was pumped hot from the copper vat and allowed to cool and settle before the addition of yeast.

Kleinman's job was really to run the business affairs, to place the orders and contract with the bottler, to pitch the beer—they called it Arlenberg's, after a cousin of Christoph Cerny's—to the local merchants, who might be prompted to stock a few bottles as a tryout. Really, it was no different from selling anything else, machine tools or ladies' watches or doctors' bags, and he spent his time almost as he had before, driving through northern Pennsylvania in the Packard with a trunk of samples behind him; but sometimes, back at the warehouse, he gazed up at the shining steel fermenting chamber and felt a bolt of panic. What in God's name had he gotten into? Everything he had was in the hands of his brewmaster. The first round of beer they made was spoiled— by bad hops, Christoph Cerny said, and Kleinman almost lost heart. He recalled in panic the smiling grain broker who had sold the goods to him at a discount. They were making lager, which required two months of aging, and in the meantime Ginger had become pregnant with Jimmy. The brewery's second and third round of bills came due well before they had produced their first good bottle of beer.

Sometimes at his desk as he closed the books and gathered up his belongings for the drive home, he contemplated his future: if the brewery failed he would be ten years paying off his debts, running valises up and down the coast while Ginger struggled to raise their children in the foundry-shadowed apartment to which they'd be forced to move. There were neighborhoods in Pittsburgh that were still covered with a dull layer of ash. He imagined his children there, running filthy through the street. Even in the womb Jimmy was docile, moving so softly beneath Ginger's belly that Kleinman could never feel the kicks himself. Ginger would wake him in the middle of the night and say sweetly, "There. No, there. Feel him?"

At those moments, at the moments when he imagined the ash gathering in the air above their house, when he imagined failure heaped upon failure, two sickly children and a middle age of debt and toil, his mind sometimes returned him to the cave on Agunijima. The sheets over his arms bound him and he struggled to free his hands. He remembered the cold rock and the tiny chime of the waterfall from deep below him in the cavern. And then the moment when he stood above his sleeping enemy, a man with children of his own perhaps. Children waiting for him to return.

Jimmy came down to the living room and said, "Asher's ready for his bedtime, Pop. Claudine thought you might want to read him a story."

"Read to him? He's not even three months old."

"We started reading to him the day he was born," said Claudine. She was at the door now, holding Asher on her shoulder.

"Before that even," said Jimmy. "I used to read out loud over her belly. He loved it."

"They're just board books," Claudine said. "Big black-and-white pictures. Just a couple of words. Babies love looking at pictures, especially of other babies."

"Excuse me," Kleinman said. "How do you know he loved it when you read to him in the womb?"

"Because whenever I did it, he kicked."

"Maybe that means he *didn't* like it."

"Sometimes I don't understand you," said Jimmy.

"Such is the nature of a human being," Kleinman answered. He stood and went to the window. "Understanding is not what this life has given us."

"Pop, what's the matter with you? It's reading. How can anything be wrong with reading?"

"What's the matter with me?" Kleinman answered. "Nothing's the matter with me. I just don't want to do it. What's the matter with everyone else?"

Kleinman's daughter, Hannah, his youngest child, took her time with everything she did. She didn't graduate from college until the summer of 1992, when she received a degree from

Bucknell in French literature. Kleinman didn't know what a young woman did with a major like that, but he decided that with three kids out of school now it was safe to begin spending the money he'd made. Harry had tenure at Rice already, and Jimmy was selling for a company that mounted museum exhibits. Kleinman had close to $10 million in brokerage accounts, and he and Ginger still lived in the same four-bedroom Tudor at the edge of Squirrel Hill (Hannah's bedroom had been added on, actually, a not so cleverly blended conversion of the upstairs porch). He cared about the $10 million and he didn't care about it. At the same time that it was the marker of all he'd accomplished, of his turning a one-in-a-thousand dream into a working business that now kept alive dozens of citizens of Allegheny County—not to mention the emblem of his ignoring all the advice he'd ever received—it was also a meaningless, even laughable, number on his monthly statements. Meaningless in that it was more than, say, a year's grocery bills, his tiny mortgage, and the last of two decades of extortive college tuition. His neighbors were dentists and accountants and the superintendent of schools, men with plenty of money but with nowhere near, he calculated, what he himself had socked away. And the real money, the money of generations, didn't start for several blocks into the neighborhood. So what? He didn't even spend it. He had an inkling that to care too much about wealth would be to invite misfortune of a more profound type.

In July of 1992 they went to Barbados. It was the wrong time of year to go, but Kleinman was inexperienced in the world of leisure and he'd wanted to go there anyway ever since childhood, when his uncle Manny, a bachelor suit-salesman from Brooklyn, used to tell him stories about walking with his girlfriend there on miles of deserted white-sand beach, implying for Kleinman's ears alone that they'd been walking au naturel. So it had always loomed for him as an exotic destination. On the map he kept in his office, Barbados was a tiny green corpuscle off the coast of South America, turned dark from where his finger had roamed over it countless times, absently, as he planned distribution in the South and East. He presented the idea to Ginger the morning after they'd driven back from Hannah's graduation, and she didn't even object. A surprise of the first order.

They flew first class, and though Kleinman expected her to object to this as well, Ginger did not even stiffen as he took her by the arm and led her up the front set of stairs to the plane. She ordered a Scotch with him when she learned it was on the house; then they rose over the city of Pittsburgh, banked, and headed south toward Miami. There they transferred to an old DC-7, sitting like a fat missile on the tarmac, its fading paint and bellowing propellers prompting both of them to order another drink as soon as they were in the air. When the island itself came into view out over the stretch of shining Caribbean, tears formed in his eyes. He gripped her hand. The dark forest of the interior rimmed by pale sand, the white of the coastal spume, then a kaleidoscope of translucent blues, whitening at the breakwater where, from a thousand feet up, he could see the meandering shadow of a huge fish over the reef. Then the sea again, endless. He turned away from the window so Ginger wouldn't see his face. The last time he'd seen an island was in the China Sea.

He had fifty years of frugality behind him and it all washed clean in an instant; perhaps it was the Scotch. At the airport he hired a private driver for the week, and at the hotel he changed rooms, to a top-floor suite with windows on three sides and vases of exotic flowers with blooms like the heads of birds. Along with the room came a cabana at seaside and a dark-haired island boy who ran back and forth from the hotel veranda offering them drinks, plates of flying fish, and whole pineapples scooped clean and filled with papaya, mango, and coconut, swimming in what tasted like peppermint schnapps or something like crème de menthe. Kleinman had never been a daytime drinker, just his Glenfiddich at supper, but here he was on some kind of a roll—he allowed himself to nibble the fruit and sip the island concoctions the boy carried over at a trot, their tiny umbrellas twirling in the wind from offshore. Ginger seemed to go along with it as well, and he had the sudden feeling that perhaps he'd missed a side of her somehow, overlooked a willingness to enjoy herself that had been hidden for fifty years; perhaps he should have brought her here sooner.

There was another couple in the cabana next to theirs, and that afternoon at the waterline Kleinman made their acquaintance. Vicky and Ray Grendine, from Palm Springs, California. Friendly people who'd been vacationing here for a dozen years. They, too, liked coming in the summer, despite the rain, because the place was empty. Ray had been in the fiberglass business in Troy, Michigan, and had been a supplier for Chris-Craft boats before he sold the factory and moved west for the weather. Kleinman looked him over and figured he was good for fifteen to twenty million—more than he himself was, the chances were; but they seemed to be on similar footing nonetheless. All such men were patriots, Kleinman had long ago discovered. Grendine had used to be Greenstein, he was told within a half-hour of meeting: Flatbush Avenue, Brooklyn, and before that Kraków. The two of them stood at the shore, gazing out at the huge sun dropping between the palms, chuckling at that one. Kleinman told him about Hannah's degree in French literature; Grendine had a daughter, too, and she'd studied art history. The two of them chuckled again, and Grendine's wife, Vicky, went over behind them to introduce herself to Ginger, while beyond them the horizon lit itself above the palms like a log about to flame.

"I guess I don't see why not, anyway," Kleinman said. "If that's what the girls like."

"That's right," said Ray Grendine. "I mean, if she likes Baudelaire, then let her study Baudelaire. What's the use of a pot of *gelt* anyway when you die?"

That night they hired a boat together and went out on the water for dinner. The crew sailed them out into a cove of reef, where the tiny marine animals lit up the seabed with their natural phosphorescence; the glow swept around them in undulating waves of light so bright that Kleinman suspected chicanery, some arrangement of flashlights tied beneath the hull or fixed to the bottom, beneath the shallow water. But it was all natural, Ray Grendine assured him; they'd seen it every year. Ginger dropped to her knees at the railing and stared into the water, unable to take her eyes off the phenomenon. There was a childlike fascination in her face that made him wish, again, that he'd brought her here sooner. He stood by the mast, watching her. And watching the cabin boy, too, for signs that they were being hoodwinked.

For dinner they ate roast goat and drank a 1959 Château Margaux that the Grendines had brought aboard, followed by a '67 Château d'Yquem with dessert. Kleinman had the distinct feeling these were expensive wines, but he was a single-malt man himself and felt enough joust left between him and Ray Grendine that he didn't want to ask. He liked the fellow, but they'd only met that afternoon. He made a note to check on the labels back home. After the meal the crew swept away the plates, brought out liqueurs, folded up the table, and disappeared, then appeared again on the foredeck with steel drums and guitars, playing island melodies. The Grendines wandered aft and began to dance while the moon rose above them; after a moment Kleinman and Ginger moved into each other's arms as well. They were not good dancers but could do a simple waltz together, which blended surprisingly well with the native music. Kleinman felt a rush of ardor and health, his wife in his embrace, the music reflected back up at them by the shallow phosphorescent coral and the ice-smooth water. Brighter than the water even was the moon climbing above the gentle arc of palms. This was what all his money was for. He had accounts at three different brokerages, but hadn't gone on a vacation in twenty years. Strange to have missed the point like that.

Near midnight, the boat dropped them at the hotel. A warm trade wind had risen and in the moonlight the spume shone as far in both directions as he could see, a great curve of white sand and sea that could have been the edge of the earth. He left Ginger in front of the hotel and went to say good night to the Grendines, who were spending the night in their cabana. They made plans to meet again in the morning, and Kleinman walked back up the still-warm sand, full of the delight of having found himself here, unexpectedly, on nothing more than a whim.

When he returned, Ginger was gone from the front of the building. On the veranda, a guard was dozing at his station, and one of the hotel peacocks approached Kleinman gingerly, roused by his footsteps, its tail feathers pulled tight. Kleinman reached for it, but it withdrew, then stood its ground and fanned its extravagant plumage. He laughed. He wished Ginger could have been with him at that moment. He wanted Hannah there, too, and Harry and Jimmy. This was what he would do: he would bring the whole family here for the holidays, every year. Harry would learn to windsurf and Jimmy would return from long walks on the beach carrying bags full of coral. Suddenly the peacock fanned its tail and made a horrifying screech. Kleinman looked around in surprise, but the guard had not been awakened. Then the bird began to make some kind of ferocious mechanical humming with its tail feathers, vibrating them like rattlers. The sound was shockingly loud. It screeched again, and he realized he had backed it into a corner. He retreated and crossed the veranda.

He rode the elevator up to their suite; but Ginger wasn't there, either. He opened the balcony doors for the breeze, changed into the hotel robe, and sat down on the bed. Hannah and Ginger could find tiny native restaurants, and art galleries where he would buy the local carvings and primitive, colorful paintings for his office. He poured himself a glass of water and ate one of the tiny plums that he found in a basket by the bed. Still Ginger hadn't returned, and after a time he went to the balcony rail to look for her. The beach was empty, but his view was broken by the thickly dotted palms. He slipped back into his sandals and walked downstairs. The guard station was deserted. The restaurant was closed, and in the lounge the barman was drying tumblers with a dish towel. He hadn't seen her, either. Kleinman moved out onto the sand, which was empty now in both directions. He walked quickly to the Grendines' cabana, but the light there was extinguished. He knocked lightly, and Ray Grendine came to the thatched window in his robe. He'd seen no sign of her, either, though he remembered watching her walk north along the water while Kleinman had been saying good night to them earlier.

Kleinman set off. The peacock came down from the veranda and followed him a short distance, like a bully, then lost interest. Kleinman walked briskly. He wanted to look everywhere, but the palms made a thicket of shadows. His progress was slow. The wind was warm and the sea ruffled, but it was gentle as a lake; it seemed unlikely that any harm had come to her. But then he thought of the crew on the boat, or perhaps one of the cabana hands; worse yet, the local boy who that afternoon had swum up every few minutes to the hotel beach, climbed quickly from the water, and sprinted to the cabanas to offer the guests woven hats and shell necklaces from a plastic pouch before the guard chased him back into the water. He was a ragged-looking child, really, now that he thought of it. And perhaps not even a child. The glint in his eyes as he showed his palmful of trinkets was far from the friendliness

Ginger had called it. He shuddered. He should never have let her out of his sight. How had such a miscalculation occurred? He thought back: she had been with him climbing down from the boat, assisted through the warm shallows by one of the crewmen, who had held her sandals up over his head. That was the last he remembered. Then, Ray Grendine said, she had set off up the beach. Now he was letting his imagination get ahead of him. Perhaps she had merely lain down to rest beneath one of the palms. He checked the shade of every trunk, winding his way north along the water. Eventually he came to the end of the hotel grounds, where a wall of rocks had been piled as a border. Now he was indeed afraid. This was what happened if you spent your money cravenly. If you let down your guard. It seemed unlikely that she would have gone over the wall of rock, but he climbed it anyway, holding on to the warm stones with his hands, moving steadily up until at the top he stood looking out over the jumbled peak toward the windward shore of the island.

Then he turned to the sea, and that is when he saw her, not five yards away from him, sitting on the wall looking up at the moon. Her back was turned, and when he approached and laid his hand on her shoulder, she let out a tiny gasp. "It's me," he said. "Your husband of the last half-century."

Walking back up the beach, he told her of his plans, of bringing Hannah and Harry and Jimmy here for the holidays, of taking regular family vacations together the way their neighbors did in Squirrel Hill, trips to Jamaica and the Virgin Islands and the Outer Banks of North Carolina.

In front of the hotel he stopped, but Ginger kept on walking.

He came up after her, turned her around, and pointed up at the light still shining on their balcony. "Which hotel did you think it was?" he asked her, pointing up the empty beach.

~~~~~~

B y the early fifties, business was booming. By now he had a distribution network and a comfortable arrangement with the Teamsters, who trucked Arlenberg's east to Newark, west to Cincinnati, and as far south as the Florida Keys. He had two secretaries in the office and money in the bank and was contemplating the purchase of a home at the edge of Squirrel Hill, where he and Ginger took the children for strolls on Sunday afternoons. One day at closing time in January of 1953, a phone call came after both secretaries had gone home.

"August Kleinman?"

"Speaking?"

"Meyer Sharp wants a meeting with you."

"Who?"

"Meyer Sharp."

"Who's Meyer Sharp?"

"Five forty-five P.M. at the promontory at the lock, six miles south of your establishment."

"Five forty-five? That's in half an hour! Who's Meyer Sharp?"

"Don't be late. And be alone."

It was like a gangster movie. He descended the stairs from his office to the tun, where Christoph Cerny was tending to the heat-ing of a new batch of mash. He told him about the phone call. Christoph Cerny said, "Don't go."

"Why? Do you know this Meyer Sharp?"

"Never heard of him."

"Then why do you tell me not to go?"

"I know the type of man. You don't need a man like that."

"A man like what? It's not an Italian name."

"With all due respect," Christoph Cerny said. "I would suggest you do not go."

"All right," Kleinman said. "Thank you for your advice."

He'd heard of men like Meyer Sharp before, of course—an oddity he'd discussed recently at dinner, that it was not just Italians in the Mob but Jews, too. He should have been afraid, but instead he was annoyed. He walked out to the Lincoln, cursing the wind as he struggled with his coat. It was bitter cold and the river was half in ice. The whole barren landscape made him angry: the stripped trees, the swirling leaves, the small-time hood, Meyer Sharp, who was out to rock the boat. Whoever this Meyer Sharp was, he would set him straight.

Or they could make a simple, peaceful deal. If it required some money, he had it now to give. Business to business. The land south of the brewery changed quickly nearing Pittsburgh: dead-end roads and crumbling docks and the shells of old mining operations stripped of their gears and belts; locks and dams along the river where the water tumbled, gradually changing color until it was brown from the slag; barges floating low with ore. The promontory overlooked a lock on a narrow section of the river, an unused gangway of asphalt over a bouldered peninsula that jutted over

the water at a swift double bend. From the road he could see Pittsburgh. There was a pump house at the end of the promontory, and
when Kleinman crossed the parking lot, a man stepped out from
behind it. Again like the movies. The light was failing. He didn't
like the idea of a meeting at the end of a narrow catwalk over the
frigid water, but still he wasn't afraid. At worst he would end up in
a deal. He walked out to the tip.

As soon as the man set foot on the gangway, Kleinman saw that
he was an idiot. A narrow temple, too narrow for a human being's,
like the skull of a racing dog. Features that were not features. A
lack of wrinkles. Skin shiny, as if it had been chemically cured.
Cheap black overcoat over an insignificant body. One hand in the
pocket. This indicated a pistol. Kleinman said, "Where's Meyer
Sharp? I'll talk to Meyer Sharp."

"You're talking to him."

"Excuse me? *You're* Meyer Sharp!"

"You're going to give me a piece of your business."

Now the hand rose a few inches in the pocket. But a flicker of
underconfidence moistened the expressionless eyes. Kleinman
saw it in the fading light, just before the man turned. This was not
Meyer Sharp. No Meyer Sharp looked like this—this was an im-
postor. How did Kleinman know? He just did. Thank God for his
years in sales. The man kept his back to him, stepped up to the
rail. A gesture designed to show fearlessness. Kleinman understood this, also from his years in sales. He could see the weight of
the pistol in the overcoat. The water, flung around the outside
curve of the rapids, swirled fifty feet below, bobbing with bathtub-
sized chunks of ice. Kleinman glanced across at the empty lot.

Then he crouched and drove his body forward, shoulder lowered, so that on impact the man flew over the rail, grunting like an expelling balloon, turned once in the air waving his arms, and went crashing down into the rapids.

His head surfaced for a moment, but then the river took him. It sucked him down into the dark swirls in which the great blocks of ice dunked him and turned him over in their run for the deep channel in the middle. The head disappeared.

Kleinman scrambled down the embankment to the shore. From this close, the bumping and twirling ice made a low screech, as though somewhere out on the dark water a piece of heavy machinery were turning its gears. But it was just the colliding floes. He called feebly out into their rumbling: "Mr. Sharp! Hey, Meyer Sharp!" The water churned by. "Hello! Hey, Meyer Sharp!" He ran back up the hill again but could see nothing. The glowing furnace stacks downriver gave him no view but of their own chopped reflections on the waves. He was breathing ferociously. Suddenly he was seized with terror that he hadn't actually killed the man. That as he waited looking into the dark, his assailant was climbing from the water and coming to find him.

He drove home. He parked around back, went inside, locked the doors, and shut off all the lights. He collected Ginger and Harry and Jimmy, gathered some documents from his filing cabinet, and took all of them to the Lincoln. Then he went back inside for a moment to turn on an upstairs light and the television. On the road north, as soon as the kids fell asleep, he explained to Ginger what had happened. His hands shook on the wheel. From a motel in New Jersey he phoned his attorney, an ex-detective from the Pittsburgh police. He gave no details of what had occurred, just asked him to research a name. The next evening, the attorney called him back in Boston. There was no Meyer Sharp in the local Mob. Had Kleinman got the name wrong? No, the name was Meyer Sharp. He'd heard it twice distinctly.

Well, there was no such figure. Nowhere on the eastern seaboard.

What did that mean? He called Christoph Cerny, told him he was going to be away for a few days for an illness in Ginger's family, then stayed on in Boston at the Copley Hotel, mulling his choices. Ginger wanted to go to her relatives in the North End, but Kleinman absolutely forbade it. He needed time to think. If there was no Meyer Sharp, then who was the thug? And what had Kleinman done to him? Was this murder? Clearly, there had been a firearm in the man's hand. But nonetheless—would such a fact save him in court? When the body washed up, rose out of the melting ice in spring or flattened itself against one of the intake ports at a foundry, would he begin a tormenting ordeal? The desire to confess was overwhelming. There were two parts to this desire: guilt was one, and it surprised him. Brought back his memories of standing in a dark cave in the East China Sea. But this man was nothing more than a goon; the slick face perhaps suggested retardation. He certainly had no family, no children waiting for him as it grew dark above the city. But perhaps he had. Perhaps Kleinman had misunderstood. He felt a physical pain, a dull prod low in the gut that would not go away. Heartache. He was sweating all the time. The other part of the desire to confess was his belief that going to the police before they came to him might reduce the criminal consequences of his act.

But perhaps there had been no crime at all. Perhaps the man had crawled out of the river at the sandbar that was formed every year by the turn of rapids. Perhaps he was sitting in a car right now outside Kleinman's house, waiting for the flicker of the TV to vanish from the window.

He resolved not to weaken on such an urgency. Besides, he had lived long enough in Pittsburgh and New York that he no longer took comfort in the authorities. He would wait it out. He had a good lawyer and a visible place in the community. Every day he called in to work, kept himself abreast of the state of business affairs, inquired casually about calls that might have come in for him or about visitors at the plant. But nothing happened. No unusual messages arrived. Mrs. Oxenbridge opened his mail and there was nothing out of the ordinary. And as the days passed up north, he began to grow a bit more steely. The incident itself took on a slight vagueness. The actual details began to crowd themselves. Why had he been so sure there was a gun? Might it have been something else? What words had been exchanged? He resolved to wait further. Each morning he woke to diminishing pain in his gut. Each morning he called his lawyer. There had been nothing in the papers and no rumors down at the station, no incident involving a Meyer Sharp. The steeliness grew.

Finally, they drove home again. He was a businessman with responsibilities, a veteran of the war. He'd killed a man, perhaps, but it was in self-defense and in defense of his business, which was also the livelihood of a good number of citizens of Allegheny County. He went over his options. He could still go to the police with the story, slightly changed: it had been a deflection of Meyer Sharp's lunge at him. But why would a man with a pistol lunge? Or he could head back to New England permanently, find a new life for the four of them and never return. This became his preference for a time, but Ginger, surprising him, told him it was not an option. You did not run from men like this, she told him, drawing on a knowledge that strengthened his suspicions about her relatives in Boston. His instinct told him there was no Meyer Sharp at all, that the man had merely been trying to swindle him into a few months of payments. He recalled the slightly moistened eyes, the idiot's features. Well, if indeed there was a Meyer Sharp, he'd soon find out.

Back home, the first thing he did was buy life insurance. Then he organized a party. He rented a paddle wheeler and served dinner on the Ohio for 250 guests, stood near the rail himself as often as he could so that any one of them—they were beer and delivery kings from up and down the coast—could come for him if that was what they wanted to do; they could struggle at the rail and be done with it. Or, if needed, they could shoot him from shore— this thought did not escape him. He turned his profile against the light of the pilothouse. Let it be now or never, boys. The dinner was staggeringly expensive, but this was a business investment. He wanted it to be clear that he was staying in Pittsburgh as the man in charge at Arlenberg's. No two-bit player with an animal's skull was going to run him out of town. He was terrified, but that didn't stop him. He had a life to lead in Pittsburgh. He didn't want to be looking over his shoulder.

~~~~~~~~~~~~~~~~~~~~~~~~~~~~~~~~~~~~~~

H e went out onto the porch to plant a few bulbs in the long pots and look out at the lights across the river. The Brooklyn Bridge—it was more beautiful to him than all the paintings in the world. It shone, twice-reflected, in the dark water, its lights an inverted, glittering arch in one direction and the moon shadows of its cables a dark ghost in the other. A dinner yacht disappeared beneath the span, then appeared again as it made its way up the center of the East River. The planter boxes were filled with some kind of climbing ivy, but despite the dense leaves, the stems were sparse; between them, four across in each pot, he dug and set a dozen tulips. The velvet sack was still half-full of bulbs when the door opened behind him. Jimmy said, "What are you doing, Pop? Burying nuts?"

"I'm just getting rid of some flowers of your mother's."

"Are you all right?"

"Perfectly," said Kleinman. "These are Dutch bulbs. The best. Christoph Cerny brought them back for your mother."

"And you're putting them in *here*?"

"What else am I supposed to do with them?"

"I don't know," Jimmy said. "How about throw them out?"

"Out of the question. The whiskey, maybe"—he held up the

velvet sack, which once had contained a bottle of Crown Royal that he'd received as a gift—"but never the bulbs."

"Well, I hope they like car exhaust then." Jimmy sat on the rail and looked at his father. "Hey, Pop," he said gently. "I was only kidding. They'll do fine here. Lots of sun. And Claudine loves flowers, too. So do I—"

"Don't humor me."

"Look, I didn't mean what I said tonight. About *yahrzeit* for Mom. I didn't know—"

"That's all right," Kleinman said. "I don't know what happened to me, either." He dug a trench with his fingers, coaxed another bulb from the sack, set it upright in the hole. "You're right. I don't believe in any of those religious things. I was just feeling sorry. I miss your mother. It was the time of the evening. I've always felt something when the sun goes down."

Jimmy was silent. Finally, he said, "Claudine suggested I should come outside here with you. Would you rather be alone?"

Kleinman turned to look at him, silhouetted by the thicket of lights on the East Side of Manhattan. Jimmy had always been peculiar in the manner in which he was swayed by others. Sometimes he was stubborn as an ox—Kleinman recognized himself—but at other times he was docile in a worrisome way. Where did this come from? Kleinman couldn't tell him anything, but Claudine seemed to be able to tell him when to sneeze. "No, no. Of course I want you out here."

"So, how is everything in Boston, Pop?"

"Fine. Decent."

"What do you do these days?"

"I work," Kleinman said. "I listen to good music. I walk."

"And how are you feeling?"

"Perfect. No problems there."

"I mean, how are you feeling about your life?"

"About my life?" That's what Jimmy was like. For years on end words failed him. Then suddenly there were too many of them. "Sad," Kleinman said. "I'm feeling sad." He set another bulb in a hole. "But I'm seeing someone."

Jimmy said, "Who?"

"Isabela."

"Isabela?"

"She's West Indian. Works at the Bread and Circus too. Has a five-year-old daughter. Name Aida."

"Christ, Pop. How old is she?"

"I would never ask."

"She must be half your age. At most. You're going to kill yourself. Are you taking your pills?"

"Don't worry, it's not that. I could give two beans about that. We take walks. That's all."

"Is it serious?"

"Don't worry, the will is long written. You kids get everything. But who knows? Maybe that's not good. I got nothing."

"Pop, I wasn't worried."

"Yes, it's serious. She's very lovely."

The door opened. Claudine said, "Time for bed, sweetheart. Services are at six-thirty." Then it closed again.

"Coming," said Jimmy.

"What?" said Kleinman. His son seemed pleased to have orders. "You're really going to services again?"

"They're not bad, actually," Jimmy said. "Kol Nidre was nice. We just go twice on Yom Kippur. Not the whole day or anything."

"Excuse me, but that's three times. Three times seems like a lot to me. Especially for someone who doesn't believe in it."

"It's really not bad," said Jimmy. "It's a Renewal congregation. And I never said I didn't believe in it."

"Excuse me again, but what is a revival congregation?"

"It's an offshoot of the Chasids, believe it or not. Claudine found it. It's mostly music. It's very beautiful, actually. Not what you'd think. And it's *Renewal*, not revival."

"Music? Sounds to me like you're going to a church. For me, no thank you. I've had enough black magic in my life."

"Why don't you give it a try, Pop?"

"Give it a try?" Kleinman turned his back, looked again across the river at the low end of Manhattan Island, where the ceaseless trade of the new immigrants ran day and night, unabated, meat trucks and cabs and delivery vans scrabbling furiously over the pocked-up roads. That would have been his own life if he'd stayed with what he'd been offered. Tallithim and haftarah, the incessant mumbling of prayer and argument. The scraping commerce. He'd given it plenty of try. It wasn't the religion; it was accepting what was given you. This was the gravest of sins.

"What do you say, Pop?"

"I say, No thank you."

"Well, don't think I've finished about Isabela," Jimmy said. Then he went inside. As the door closed, Kleinman heard, "Sorry, love—sorry, sorry, sorry."

Hannah was their midlife child, an astonishment to Kleinman but not, apparently, to Ginger, who was forty-two in 1966 when Hannah was born, and benignly undisturbed by the turn in their lives, as though she'd known forever of the preposterous surprise of it. For years she'd wanted a daughter. Kleinman suffered silently from the lack of sleep. Harry was at Penn by then and Jimmy a junior in high school, that fall immersed in one of his long periods of sour quiet. But nonetheless he took right away to Hannah. Watching Jimmy sit on the couch with his newborn sister in his arms, Kleinman couldn't help thinking of himself with Izzy, then of his own childhood in Wavecrest and Hamburg, then that the universe indeed repeated itself. Cycles of devotion, tragedy, idiosyncrasy, and outrage: that was how the world turned. Hannah, at three years old, reached her hands one morning to both her ears and tugged distractedly at the lobes. Kleinman pulled her arms away.

Three children! Three mysteries to him! Harry, the first, somehow the natural culmination of all that he'd presumed—an energetic boy, a breaker of rules. He stood early in his crib and shook the bars. At eleven months he managed to shake the thing away from the wall and across the room, until only the narrowness of the nursery door halted him. Otherwise he would have been down the hall and to the stairs. At a year, he liked to hold a ball in his hands—a baseball, signed by Ralph Kiner, from Forbes Field: there it was in the crib, day and night. Without understanding so, Kleinman felt the pleasure of assuredness. His own bloodline, Harry seemed, stretching back. Kleinman's maternal ancestry speaking to him: *Smart you got out of the luggage business. Do something by yourself.* Harry refused meals when Ginger gave them, ate ravenously when he was supposed to be asleep. All right, Kleinman thought: do things your own way. *Take the advice of no one.* This was 1949. The brewery was teetering.

Then Jimmy, a year later. Arlenberg's was still a one-tank operation then, and the Gerstein family considered their investment to be at a precipice; but Kleinman in his own mind had begun to think of expanding. Sherman Gerstein met him every other week for lunch, his shoe tapping beneath the table. Kleinman understood the terms: twelve months to break even or the stake was withdrawn. The river tumbled past. All Kleinman had were a few words, barman rumors that the recent immigrants in the mills enjoyed the new lager. But the tavern owners were caught in a lock from the distributors. This was what Kleinman's work had become, day and night—trying to get them to give him a break. And suddenly Ginger was pregnant with their second. What could Kleinman say? In the pinging of the mash tun's burners, he heard Sherman Gerstein's tapping foot.

More than anything else, Jimmy was not Harry. A boy with a sedate expression, a smile so rare that Kleinman became antic in its pursuit. He would puff his cheeks for Jimmy, flap his arms like birds' wings, emit all manner of pops and grunts, tickle his toes, while Jimmy stared back incuriously, a monklike evasion shadowing his face. Kleinman felt withered. He sought refuge in work. This had its payoffs, gradual as they were. By the time Jimmy was six months old, Arlenberg's had caught on at a single, windowless, hill-bottom tavern that was far behind in its bills; the big breweries stopped delivering there and Kleinman—it was his only advantage—stepped into the breach. He left out the details but told Sherman Gerstein that a second copper tank had been ordered, was ready for the barge ride down the Allegheny. He fully expected Gerstein to pull the plug, but when he hesitated, Kleinman seized the opportunity; the next day he in fact ordered the tank he had mentioned. Sherman Gerstein wrote another check, loudly questioning his judgment. Failure appeared to have been staved off. This, like the war, was a lesson.

At home, he took to tossing Jimmy in the air. Ginger scolded him. He was too young for it and invariably cried after two tosses. But there was the first. The flight upward, the surprised leap of the hands, the mouth an O. It was the only reaction Kleinman could get out of him, and it seemed, if not joyful, at least interested. He wanted to be able to toss him twice without him crying. One morning Ginger said, "If you hurt him, I am taking them both with me." Kleinman laughed. "Hurt him?" Harry watched, three years old, climbing on a chair. He jumped to the floor and landed on his feet. Jimmy, in his father's hands, cried terribly until Ginger took him. Always, Kleinman tried the second toss.

It was two more years before he really understood that his boys were going to be different from each other. By then, Arlenberg's was prospering. Harry was five and riding a bicycle and swinging on the tether rope he'd planted in the center of the backyard. Jimmy remained behind. He stood in the corners of rooms; waited at the top of the stairs for his mother to lift him; ate what he was given. With the insistence of expectation, Kleinman still tossed him now and then to see if anything had changed; but it was predictable now, and Jimmy accepted the sudden flight with a neutral expression. He rose and fell like a leather sack, then turned his head to the side, searching out his mother.

He hadn't planned to tell Claudine and Jimmy about Bread & Circus. A team member! Ha! If he'd had teams at the brewery, they'd have cleaned him out forty years ago. No team role for him. Just one job. (He'd negotiated—all he had on his side was age, but this turned out to be enough.) He was a bagger. And good at it: at the bottom of the bag went juices, canned food, and boxes; next up, bulk-bin items, little shock absorbers in their plastic sacks; then vegetables; then fruit. Such an obvious simplicity, but not everyone truly took it to heart. People liked handles, too. Another obvious courtesy. After a while, the old folks were choosing his line on purpose. Got home without their groceries crushed. Do things right.

And Isabela!

He liked the rhythm. Right hand inside the bag; left hand to the conveyor; here a moment for conversation, a respectful compliment or a nod of the chin; toss left to right; then down. Now and then he saw someone he recognized. This was always good for a laugh, but they all knew he didn't need the money. Some thought he was crazy. (He could tell: the glance back on leaving.) Others, he could see, were envious.

And it was as though he'd known Isabela his entire life. Thirty-eight years old—he'd asked the team leader—with a beautiful five-year-old, Aida, and no husband. He gave her his paycheck; she hugged him. He gave it to her the next time; she hugged him again. He took Aida for walks around the block, but the girl didn't really take to him. Walked looking down at the sidewalk. Back in the store, she ran to her mother. He cut down his shift length so he could work six days a week instead of five. That was how you made a life.

But the feelings he had for Isabela—they took him unawares. More than anything else, they were unseemly. He spoke to Ginger: *It's not what you're thinking.*

What is it then?

He paused. *It is my memory of you and the children.*

And that indeed was what it was. At the end of his third month, he signed over another paycheck to Isabela, and that evening she asked him to walk her home. At the door to her building, a once-grand, marble-fronted mid-rise, through whose lobby doors Kleinman saw a chipped and crumbling atrium, she asked him up for a cup of tea. Not being one to presume, he accepted. The building was a prewar powerhouse that had gone down with the neighborhood. Linoleum peeking through worn carpet in the en-

tranceway. An elevator but no bulbs in the floor indicators. Clang-
ing laundry at the ends of the halls. They climbed four flights to
her apartment door, which was fitted with a row of metal-flanged
locks. A small place, but cheery from the sunlight and the obvious
inborn gentility of its occupant. Rows of small paintings over a
bricked-up mantel: beach scenes in primitive colors, none of them
framed—perhaps the work of Isabela herself. Kleinman recognized the presence of refinement amid trying circumstances. Bolts
of colorful cloth hanging from the walls. A fraying chair covered
with a deep burgundy throw. There was a grace and intelligence to
this woman—he'd spotted it months ago, buying an apple.

From outdoors came the smell of cooking. Kleinman sniffed
the air, and Isabela ran to shut the windows. When she returned,
Aida had disappeared into the back of the apartment. Then Isabela herself disappeared while Kleinman stood examining the
paintings. They were various but all done by a single hand—he
could see that now; some euphonic sense of bright color. A tropical palette but not unlike Morandi in its illumination. Perhaps he
should offer to buy one. Then suddenly Isabela appeared again,
through a narrow door he'd thought was a closet. Now she was
wearing a dark dress. With a start, Kleinman realized it was sheer.
She approached, shifted her weight to one leg, and, standing before him, asked if he cared for a drink. He felt a draw in his viscera:
he was supposed to kiss her now. He'd given her those paychecks.

"Well, no," he said. "That's not what I meant by this—"

"Downstairs is the bodega—"

"No, no—"

"I could go for wine—" she said. "Perhaps Scotch whiskey—"

"I mean, that's not how I see you. You are a beautiful girl—a very beautiful woman. But I love my wife."

"Oh," she said. "I thought—"

"Don't tell me what you thought! I love my wife. And I'm too old. I gave you the money because I don't need it. I'll give you more—"

"Oh, you are of angels."

"No. No. That's a laugh! The last thing from one."

"Yes, of angels," she said. "Of heavenly angels."

~~~~~~~~~~~~~~~~~~~~~~~~~~~~~~~

For Jimmy's second birthday, Ginger's parents came out from New York. There was a barbecue in the backyard. Harry swinging on the tether rope like a dervish and diving in the dirt. Begging to toss the ball with Ginger's father. The old man indulged him a few times, but his sight and joints were failing, and he had the foreigner's stiffness with baseball. He was wearing white trousers and white shoes, an expensive cardigan. Immigrant, but a different kind from Kleinman's people. Yet the same hawkishness in the face: probably what Ginger saw in his own.

All the while, Jimmy stood on the porch. Kleinman knew that the old man was eyeing him. Finally, Kleinman said, "Come on down here, Jimmy. Come play ball with your grandfather."

Jimmy didn't move. He was watching his mother at the stove through the glass door to the kitchen. The baseball rolled by the barbecue, and Kleinman picked it up. "Come on down and play ball with your grandfather." Ginger waved her finger at him from the stove, mouthed words through the glass: *leave Jimmy alone.*

"Come on, Jimmy. Come on down and play ball." Now the old man was saying it, too.

"Don't make me say it again," Kleinman said. He turned and whispered to the old man, "He's afraid of—"

What happened next? A sound like a quivering bow. Kleinman turned back. The door frame was shuddering. Jimmy was inside the kitchen, looking back at them. Like a framed photograph. The glass was gone. Then blood. Kleinman leapt. My God. My God. Shrieking. Ginger, turning, her hand to her mouth. Kleinman yanking Jimmy up in his arms. Blood from his hair. Ginger screaming. The glass in two pieces under his feet. The old man shouting, *"Premilo! Premilo!"*

At the hospital, Jimmy took a dozen stitches. Stared up at his father defiantly. Did not cry for the procedure. A two-year-old not crying. This was a turning in the boy's life, not unlike the war had been for Kleinman. The nurse said, "That's some gentleman there," as she taped the sutures when the doctor was finished. They had shaved his head for it. The tiny scalp without wrinkles. In the waiting room, an old man said, "You've got a tough little boy there, sonny."

A tough little boy there. A certain erratic hardness to his character, a glimpse of the future. Jimmy loved the bandage. Didn't want to take it off even after a week, when the sutures were pulled. Even after the hair had begun to grow in. At the doctor's, he'd asked his mother to retrieve the pulled dressing from the nurse so he could bring it home. A two-year-old walking around with a bloody wad of gauze in his pocket. To Kleinman it was an emblem. He found himself picking Jimmy up now all the time but not throwing him anymore; carrying him while the little hands fingered the bandage. How did you know what your children would become? One day Harry took the bandage from him and cut it in two. Kleinman couldn't console Jimmy; even Ginger couldn't. Jimmy cried and cried.

G inger came to the patio window. "There's someone at the door wants to speak to you."

They had flown back from Barbados that very morning, darker prints of themselves, the smell of sun and lotion in their skin. Kleinman had never felt so healthy in his life. He'd brought their suitcases into the house, then gone out and stood in the backyard looking out across the neighborhood. The gardener had been there that morning and the breathing of the grass trimmings gave the air a hint of water. He counted his lucky stars to be leading such a life. Barbados in the morning. His own lawn in the afternoon, blue-green in the low sun. "Who is it?" he called back to Ginger.

"I don't know, Aug."

He looked at his wife. No alarm on her face, simply a blank expression. "Well, what does he look like?"

"A man. He looks like a man."

"Does his face look tight?"

"What?"

"Shiny?"

"It's just a man asking for you."

Kleinman went quickly inside and up the stairs to the front bedroom, but when he peeked onto the porch from the window, it was only Syd Brady, their neighbor next door. Kleinman hurried down and opened the door. Syd was dropping off a box that had been delivered to their house. "Everything all right with Ginger?" he asked.

"Yes, why?"

"Nothing, really. Tell me, do I look different to you these days?"

How had his relations with his son become what they were? They were cordial enough now but nonetheless treacherous: Jimmy could turn on him without warning; or worse, turn *away*, retreat into some memory of injustice that first silenced him and then, a moment later, shadowed his countenance. From where did those feelings spring? Kleinman couldn't say. Speaking to Ginger once, before Jimmy and Claudine were married, he had mentioned his puzzlement. She had looked back at him, equally puzzled. "Of course," she said. "It's just what you had with your own father."

This was a piece of information that had been withheld from

him. The obviousness was crushing. It seemed that there must be a second self, a hippogriff of meanness, all the time operating from its hereditary hiding place inside of him. He had shown Jimmy nothing but generosity. There'd been no linen deliveries for this boy; no banishment to the upstairs rooms while downstairs the guests drank brandy and ogled the young sopranos; no sourness and dark quiet at breakfast. And yet here it was, a generation later: a boy with the same feelings for Kleinman as Kleinman had harbored for his own father. Life was a mirror, the generations reflecting one upon the other.

When Jimmy was in junior high school, Kleinman had taken him camping once in the Poconos. The two of them grilled hamburgers and slept in a borrowed tent, and he found himself performing acts he remembered from the days with his amiable stepfather in Queens: casting his arm over his son's shoulders as they walked; picking him up in the swimming hole and throwing him upward with a shove of his knee—it was miraculous that a motion of Hank Kleinman's he remembered from the beach at Rockaway would now reproduce itself in his own limbs, his son now windmilling his arms in the northern Pennsylvania light and back-flopping into the shimmering water. Jimmy surfaced with the same delight he himself used to feel: the surprise of flight and the brace of chill water when Hank Kleinman propelled him into the surf. Jimmy, momentarily forgetting the difficulty in their relations, crossed the stream and came at him fresh, spewing water from his mouth and wrestling in the chilly current until Kleinman turned him again—it seemed that Jimmy desired to be vanquished—and propelled him upward for another dive.

But back at home the hidden assassin's tool once again went to work. The ease vanished. In high school, Jimmy took umbrage at the tone of Kleinman's voice. This was 1967, and Jimmy's hair that fall reached to his shoulder blades. Kleinman himself was suspicious enough of conformity but nonetheless found himself adopting an offended stance. He ended up needing a go-between; had to work through Ginger to ask him things—How was school? When was he planning to mow the grass? He even asked Harry to be the translator—Harry, who was at Penn by then, agreeable but distracted at vacation time, long-haired as well but with an athletic body that bespoke a basic conservatism, counting the hours until he could be back in the dormitory with his friends. Harry went along with his father, and when he talked to his brother, it was as though they had called in a gifted specialist—a speaker of the foreign tongue that was used by the sullen, unrecognizable boy in their kitchen, standing there in the light of the overhead fixture like a bushman come out of the jungle into a clearing.

On a cold May morning of his seventy-fourth year he packed the Lincoln with a lunch bag full of cheese-steaks and a cooler full of root beer and drove the two of them north to their new life. In the car, the Elgar cello concerto played.

Boston. *I should have listened when I could have.* Ginger had slept in the backseat, buttressed by pillows, her mouth occupied in forming the shape of an O, whose sound she repeated in a murmur at changing intervals as Kleinman sped north on the turnpikes. It was the *oh* of surprise; the *oh* of understanding. He hoped it wasn't the *oh* of alarm.

Retiring from the brewery had been easy; Christoph Cerny was five years gone by then, anyway, and the young man who had replaced him considered Kleinman a cantankerous old patriarch. That was obvious enough. Kleinman had asked the neurologist if Boston would help; he looked at Ginger and shrugged—not a doctor anymore but just another man, almost Kleinman's age, looking at the demise of a human being. "Sure," he said. "Why not?" They arrived midday after a night in a motel in Connecticut; the city greeted them with its shiny, brick-colored light, the stimulating clear of the day after a rainstorm.

Kleinman approached on Memorial Drive, made a wide loop, and circled back slowly on Storrow to take in the water from all angles: the reassuring cut of river bisecting settlement, the way it did in all the towns he had known. Cars honked—he remembered this from his earlier trips. *This is where you always wanted to live.* Ginger perked up, sat in the front seat watching the streets roll past. They turned away from the river and wandered through the Back Bay. The well-kept brick fronts. The swans like bright white stonework in the dark pond on the Common. By telephone Kleinman had purchased a substantial, shingled Edwardian in Newton with level, well-cut grounds. But he was in no hurry to get there.

Rosa had arrived the day before, Mrs. Fielding would be coming that weekend, and Ray DiGranza had agreed to fly up every Thursday afternoon to give his lessons. Kleinman had paid stiff sums to finance these moves, but he would have gladly paid more.

Rosa had a grandson in high school in Newark, New Jersey, and Kleinman took on the burden of his college tuition. Mrs. Fielding wanted a flight back to Pittsburgh every other weekend. This he arranged, and he doubled both their salaries. Money, money, money. Ray DiGranza only flew first class. Kleinman had a tall wooden fence installed around the yard in Newton, had the house repainted a bright barn-siding red, so that it would be unmistakable. A spa was installed and a grand garden planted, with perennials and vegetables and bulbs. The guest house was refinished for Rosa and a new bathroom added to one of the children's bedrooms in the main house for Mrs. Fielding, next door to where Ginger would sleep. Between Ginger's room and his own, a door was cut—though Kleinman had the rueful suspicion it might never be opened. Intercoms were rigged up everywhere on the grounds. All this was arranged with a telephone and a checkbook. He could buy everything but the one thing he most wanted.

I t was the war more than anything else that changed Kleinman's politics—it wasn't his wealth, which came later. This was a source of pride in his middle age, when he was something of an outcast at parties, because it seemed to him that a change in politics because of money—whether earning it or losing it—was of the most suspect heritage. So here he was in 1948, on the verge of fortune but unaware of it, suspecting bankruptcy in every envelope from his creditors and every dark sedan that appeared in the gravel lot alongside Arlenberg's—when suddenly Henry Wallace, the Progressive candidate for president, caught his attention. Why? The man was a Gentile—not just a Gentile, a religious Christian!—and he certainly promised nothing for a businessman. But the populist, Harry Truman, even with his Fair Deal, still smacked to him of the war; and the war in Kleinman's mind was a dark puzzlement—unsolved, festering. The atomic bomb might have been exploded at cloud level instead. Or in Hiroshima alone. In his gut he hated the Japanese, but was suspicious of the feeling. What, really, were the forces involved? The Russians, he understood, had been poised to invade Japan. Dreams plagued him. Confinement, savagery, the closure of rock; sometimes the roaring tumble of the landing craft. He remembered a feeling, first visited upon him when he spied the Golden Gate Bridge from the deck of the troopship on his return from the Pacific: that he had been caught up in a repugnant dynamism in which human life was dust, windborne chaff with which to cover the earth. Hank Kleinman, the pacifist, weeping on his return. Now the feeling was Kleinman's also. As his wealth grew, so did his conviction—a contradiction, but nonetheless strongly felt: the malignancy of international capital was what moved the world. A strange philosophy for a businessman and a war hero, but that was what he felt, and in his adult life he had never kept himself silent. Hiss was the hero; Whittaker Chambers the villain. In his present circles this was, needless to say, an unpopular belief. But the men on whose commerce he now depended, the grain merchants and Teamsters and bottle casters, the bankers, the controllers of capital with whom he soon found himself at restaurants, then in homes, then in private train-cars and on moored sailing yachts—their attitude further assured him in his convictions: They let him think what he wanted, as long as the beer was selling.

When the sixties came, the mood already seemed familiar. By then he had begun his dabbling in art—first the Bacons but soon a Mark Rothko, then a small Jasper Johns; the men with whom commerce bundled him stared, perplexed, at the walls of his living room, then moved to the bar, where fine whiskeys were available alongside a tank of Arlenberg's. Conversation declined and he understood himself to be an outcast. Still, the beer was selling, and where contracts were concerned, even delivery kings could say a few words about horizontal fields of color on a canvas. It became a source of amusement to him—how far he could stray from what was expected. Perhaps he was merely ahead of his time, if only by a few years. In 1962, when the UAW walked out on Studebaker-Packard in South Bend, Kleinman raised a glass; when the race riots burned Watts and Newark and Detroit he expressed, over Glenfiddich, sympathy—and alarm that Lyndon Johnson had brought in troops against his own countrymen. Most thought he was joking. His grandfather Morris Gertzmann had been a wealthy man but an ad hoc unionist—he paid wages that were above average and personally saw to those who became ill from the flax residue at his mills. This was as far back as Kleinman could trace his liberalism. Judaism the religion he had no use for; Judaism the culture, he did.

Then came the bombs: Chicago, Marin County, Manhattan, Cambridge. Those he knew were disgusted at the cowardice of American youth, but he himself was suspicious of such disgust.

He had been watching events, attuned to the secret play of inter-
ests: Da Nang, Dong Hoi, Operation Cedar Falls. In 1968 he gave
two thousand dollars to the Humphrey campaign so he could at-
tend a dinner in Cleveland where Lyndon Johnson was speaking
to veterans. The two thousand dollars was nothing to him.
Humphrey he favored over Nixon, but neither was to his taste.

He wore a cashmere suit for the event and drove up to Cleveland with another veteran of the Pacific war, a trucking-fleet magnate even wealthier than himself, who had to stop twice for
speeding tickets between Beaver Falls and Boardman. They were
in a Cadillac DeVille. Kleinman had strong feelings about the war
in Southeast Asia and had written to Everett Dirksen in March
about the futility of opposing a popular army. As they stopped for
a toll on the Ohio turnpike, the trucking magnate turned and
asked how much Kleinman had contributed to the Nixon campaign. Kleinman said, "You mean to the Humphrey campaign."

"No," the man said. "I mean to Nixon."

They ate chicken cutlets at round tables in a college banquet
room and listened to President Johnson's remarks about Abe Fortas, whom he had nominated to the Supreme Court, and about
Vietnam, where the bombing would go on, he promised, as long
as American lives were on the line. This was the Democratic platform. The crowd, who were drinking from their glasses during the
bits about Fortas, now raised them around the room. Kleinman,
when he looked about at the faces, felt for the first time in years
that he had been naïve: these men were giving the same amount to
Nixon! Of course. Ha! When the president was finished, the conversation turned again to business deals, and Kleinman chalked up

the experience to education and then made forays of his own with a man who owned liquor warehouses in Cleveland and Sandusky. At the conclusion of the meal, he found himself near the podium and put himself in line to meet the president. The man in front of him was making a plea about interstate shipping tariffs, and over his shoulder Johnson somehow caught Kleinman's eye. There was something there—an animal recognition—and when Kleinman's turn came and he stepped up to shake the huge hand, the president took it upon himself to squeeze him across the shoulders. A Secret Service man stepped aside for this but kept his arm near Kleinman's. "I can see you're a man who's not going to cozen me," said the president.

What was it? He was genial, but the eyes had the cold stonewall appraisal of a predatory fish. A scratch-dirt rancher from Texas and a boy off a ball-bearing boat from Dover, a quarter-century later. Somehow, social concern was mixed in there too. Johnson, strangely, seemed Jewish.

"No, Mr. President," said Kleinman.

"I knew that soon as I saw you. What's your opinion of what I said about our boys over there in Vietnam?"

"I think you should stop the bombing, sir." He drew a breath. "I think you're a coward for continuing."

The president said loudly, "Well, that's what I call a nonsense opinion," and Kleinman felt the hand of the Secret Service man on his back. The hand left him off a short distance from the tables.

But two months later he picked up the paper and read that the president had ordered a halt to the bombing of North Vietnam. In the interim, Kleinman had buckled, and mailed $500 to Nixon; now, however, he wrote Johnson a note, and sent another $1,000 to Humphrey.

~~~~~~

The day after his wife's funeral—she was buried wearing his mother's pearl necklace—he paid cash for a condominium in the Back Bay, and a week later, Starving Students moved most of his belongings from the Newton house into storage. From his new window on Gloucester Street he blinked out at the world—the society ladies strolling in their fur-collared coats, the bankers in their plain black suits. Loss hollowed him. Soon he decided Cambridge was where he should have been, out among the pretend-ruffian students in their thick-stacked heels and pointed eyeglasses of purplish black plastic. Cheap Indian restaurants, bums picking through the old pastry plates outside the coffee shops, the forgotten of the world. That's what he was now himself. He had $12 million in the bank and still felt life had cheated him. How did those two conditions exist in the same person? With panhandlers he was more than generous. But seeing them didn't change his sense of what was fair. All that he had had was taken away.

To inaugurate the beginning of the end of his life, he took up the cello. At a shop in Somerville he bought a lesser instrument, the work of a craftsman in one of the Carolinas, but let the shop owner know he might also be in the market for something more. In his hand he carried his father's Peccatte bow in its case; removed it to try the new instrument, but of course knew nothing, not even whether when he pulled it across the wound-gut strings any sound would emanate. But it did, a surprising growl from within the convex casements, the voice of a feline animal, mourning. Surprised, he nearly dropped the bow. The owner said, "Excellent tone, sir, for a beginner."

Kleinman said, "Don't worry, the sale is assured."

He took up lessons. For the scales and the required discipline he had little heart, but sometimes as he sat in his darkening condominium pulling randomly at the thick strings, the Peccatte for a moment would come alive in his fingers. Now and then he hit the resonance, and the cooperation of physics astounded him—the deep, mournful tone from his beginner's bow, the tone that contained, as he often thought while listening to Casals on his old reel-to-reel, the principles of elegy and human longing. For the first time in decades he thought of Hamburg, of the veined marble staircase that ascended from the dark atrium of his father's house toward the landing that was lit with canal light through the stained-glass windows of the balcony; the polished balustrade there sloped and curved into a tight ring of fluted walnut, which, when he came down in the early morning for school, shone in the beams of colored sun like an offering palm. Coming upstairs one morning from Newbury Street with black coffee and the *Globe*, he realized with a start that his new condominium building had the same staircase. He inquired of the manager, who shrugged. Kleinman was shaken. Memory seemed like an unfamiliar companion.

Wednesdays were his lessons. He studied with a conservatory student who had advertised on the kiosks in front of the main library. At the first lesson, he took a look at Kleinman's Peccatte bow and whistled.

"It's authentic," Kleinman said.

His teacher whistled again.

"I sold the copy in Bristol, England, and bought my passage to the new world." He held it up to the light. "I was a boy of eleven. I'm talking about 1933." He remembered his father holding up the bow the same way, admiring the elegant camber—akin in a strange bit of ontogeny to the dip of a horse's spine—and the strength of the Brazilian Pernambuco, the subtle vibrating tension that he illustrated by tapping the ivory end-pin on the mantel. Bow hairs came from the tails of male horses only, Kleinman recalled now, because of the anatomy of the horse's urine stream. That was something Isaac Gertzmann used to quote to guests after he'd had a brandy, before dessert, and taken the Montagnana from its case to show around. Kleinman had always expected the cruel trick of memory to be its demise; but instead his seemed newly invigorated. A brash young man running after him. The cello lessons were to keep busy.

They took place in his teacher's dingy apartment off Boylston Street, dark from the dusty curtains and rumbling with street noise from the window that was kept two inches open for ventilation. But the smallness of the room lent resonance to the strings, and sometimes when the teacher took the instrument himself and showed Kleinman a bowing, it was as though suddenly they were sitting in the apse of a cathedral. The reverberations of the low strings vaulted down from the ceiling and engulfed them. "Do that again," Kleinman sometimes said, just so he could feel the vibration in his bones. Music transported him. That was the right word. It brought him straight to his loss. Somehow, this was a comfort.

~~~~~~~~~~~~~~~~~~~~~~~~~~~~~~~~~~~~

When they emerged outside Narita Airport, Kleinman found to his surprise that evening had fallen; the guide made arrangements for the morning and then put him into a taxi to the Capitol Tokyu, which turned out to be a rather understated hotel but pleased him anyway. On the bed lay a stiffly starched kimono and on the floor a pair of tiny slippers; he set his bag in the closet, changed into the kimono, and went to the window. He opened it and the shrill of crickets flooded the room. The night was warm, and beyond a grove of trees, the lights of Tokyo cast a pale bowl up into the sky. "I wish you were here," he said. "I should have brought you along." He moved away from the window and began preparing for bed. "They give you a kimono and slippers." He set out his clothes for the morning, lay down on the mattress, and switched off the light. The sound of the crickets soothed him. "You would have liked it," he said softly. "Especially the kimono. The crickets, too. The slippers are too small."

Early the next morning he was awakened by a drumbeat, and when he looked out his window, he saw that the hotel was next to what looked like a shrine; alongside it, a small crowd filed up to the top of a set of steps, where they performed some kind of ritual. He managed only glimpses through the leaves: bowing, a gesture with the hands, clapping. On his room telephone he inquired and found it was a Shinto temple, the drumming a part of the morning prayer. In his warm-weather slacks and the kimono, he went outside to investigate—he wasn't sure if this was akin to walking downstairs in his pajamas, but he enjoyed the feeling of the stiff, white cotton on his arms and he didn't care what people thought of him. He had never cared, really. The crowd was a bit larger now on the steps, and the drumming seemed to arise from inside the temple. At first he stood alone at the back, but then after a time he joined the slow procession upward, and when his turn came at the front, he saw that the worshipers were not actually entering the building but stopping in the gravel court in front, throwing coins into a large wooden casket under the eaves—this was the gesture with the hands—then clapping twice. A man, noticing him, explained in excellent English that the clapping was to gain the attention of the gods. Kleinman thanked him and tried a bow, which was returned. This ritual appealed to him—all of it appealed to him, especially that the worshipers never entered the building. It was what he would have preferred himself, for the Jews. A certain distance from the trappings of idolatry. Such asceticism might have brought him back to the fold. When his turn came in line, he imitated what he had seen, threw two quarters and a newly circulated silver dollar from his pants pocket; then, as the Japanese around him had done, he clapped twice and closed his eyes as though in prayer. His feeling of reverence emerged, but he found no words coming to mind. Instead, he spoke to Ginger again. "Look at me," he said to her. "Not what you would have guessed." Then: "I wish you could have been here."

"What kind of man brings such trouble on himself or anyone else?"

"It's not trouble."

"What are you doing in Japan then? It's arrogance."

"It's not arrogance," he answered. "It's a mitzvah." He stood there as the next supplicant approached the top of the stairs. "Wait," he said. "You'll see what I mean." He watched with a certain envy as the man performed the obligations, a sureness in the movement of the hands, a calmness to the face. "And by the way," he said. "I never converted—that was a misunderstanding."

In October he had taken Ginger to a neurologist, who asked her a series of questions that left her furious, standing up off the examining table to leave. Kleinman joined in her indignation, taking her early from the appointment and treating her to lunch at Top of the Triangle instead. "Doctor?" he said after the waiter had brought his veal. "What doctor? That man had the social graces of a prison guard."

But Ginger was no longer angry. "He looked like Jimmy," she said. "That was sweet. I'll take the salad."

"That's what you ordered, my love."

When they got home, he went upstairs and called the neurologist himself, apologized for having left early. He'd heard her answers and the lack of them—the panic in her eyes when he asked her who the president was. At first he had thought she was joking, but the thin smile gave it away.

She was scheduled for tests. A CT scan. Blood work. A series of questions on the second visit, some of which Kleinman himself could not have answered ("What do you call this part on a pocket watch? The *fob*."). The doctor asked her to draw a clock, and she drew a slanting circle, no more. No hands. No numbers. "What's missing?" Kleinman said. Her anger flashed. The pencil thrown across the room. Again he took her to lunch.

Driving around Pittsburgh, he brought her past all the familiar sights. The Jewish Community Center. The plaza and the cascading fountain, cloaked in a rainbow. Squirrel Hill, and a view of all the progress that had been made in their lifetimes. When they first arrived here, the outskirts had been cloaked in a haze of industrial ash. Now the copper chimney flashings of Squirrel Hill stretched ahead of them, twinkling in the high sun. "Can you see our house from here?" he asked her, pretending that he had left his glasses at home; and to his relief she knew it right away—the brown-roofed, triple-gable Tudor three blocks ahead. "Truman was president when we bought the thing," he said. "George Bush is the president now."

The next morning, Jimmy and Claudine went to services again. Claudine wore a textured black chemise in which, turning to the mirror as she reached the front door, she suddenly brought to Kleinman's mind a picture of Ginger, the loose fabric curving delicately up at the rump. My God, he had never seen that before, the resemblance. He stared after her. So this was what Jimmy had found—a certain view, angled to the side and rear, of his mother as a young woman. Kleinman wiped his eyes. Jimmy clumped down the stairs behind him in a gray suit, and at the door he turned and said, "Everything all right, Pop?"

"Of course. Of course."

"Now remember, I have the pager and it's set to vibration, so you can page us out of services if you need to. And don't forget about Mrs. Diamond next door. You can ask her for help."

"Will you stop worrying?"

"I'm just telling you, Pop. He might cry a little, and there's no need to worry, but if you don't like what's happening, you can page us too."

"Do you think I didn't raise you?"

"I know you did. But if you need us, you can page us. That's all I'm saying."

Then the door closed and Kleinman was alone. He turned and headed for the kitchen, once again thinking of the view of Claudine from the side. The door opened again and Jimmy reached his head around. "Oh, and one more thing, I wouldn't take him outside. There's a flu around. Two babies in Queens got meningitis."

"I wouldn't dream of taking him outside."

The door closed again. Kleinman watched Jimmy disappear down the walk and around the corner. Then he went into the kitchen, sat down at the table, and glanced through the mail. There was a statement from an investment bank, unopened. He pursed the envelope to see if he could read the balance through the address window. Jimmy could make him angry like no one else on earth. Why was that? As a boy, he used to follow around his older brother, lurking at the backs of rooms, to the sides of doorways, turning up underfoot after all the neighborhood children had disappeared into the sunny afternoon. Kleinman had walked around feeling consternation for his younger boy, walked around for years wishing Jimmy the strength and gumption to lead a pack of kids on a run through the expanse of yards. There had been no adjoining lawns in Rockaway, and no timidity either. And along with Jimmy's timidity came a questioning in Kleinman's mind: was it he himself who had hurt Jimmy somehow? Given him too much? Chasing him around the yard as a two-year-old because the boy did not take naturally to any sort of physical activity—had Kleinman created the fear that held his son? Or perhaps it was simply everything Kleinman had provided. That could have been the problem, too. Those lawns. Those private schools. Those bicycles on their birthdays and, later, cars. But Harry and Hannah had known the same good fortune and not been softened by it. This was how the puzzlement turned so quickly to anger, though it shamed Kleinman to feel it. Anger at the one son ill-made for the world; anger at the one who could least withstand it. When he felt that he himself had been responsible for his son's timidity, his sorrow turned to wrath. He wasn't proud of this reaction, but there it was.

The previous night, after they'd left for services, the door had opened and Jimmy's head had appeared inside. He'd said, "And, Pop, make sure—"

But then he'd heard Claudine's voice from the garage: "Let him alone, sweetheart."

It was the look on Jimmy's face: half mastery—he was going to command his father about something—and half submission—as soon as Claudine spoke, he ducked back out the door—that brought out Kleinman's ire. He indulged it for a moment, remembering Jimmy running after Harry. Then it passed.

He set down the envelope from the bank. The kitchen was full of expensive-looking gadgets—a blender, some kind of dicer-shredder, a dishwasher covered in stainless steel. A moment later, a sound came from the monitor. He rose from the kitchen table and climbed the stairs to the nursery. Asher was on his side, propped against a triangular pillow that held him from rolling. He was still asleep, but suddenly he swung his hands together in front of his face, as if in a dream he were falling. Kleinman examined the curled, stubby fingers, the short forearms held up in front of the chest like a boxer's. Asher opened his eyes. But he didn't cry.

Kleinman said, "That's a boy. It's your Grandpop Augie."

Asher stared up at him. The feeling overwhelmed Kleinman: it was Jimmy in the crib. He looked away.

He looked back. "It's me," he said. "Your papa."

Asher made no motion.

"Your mama's in the kitchen," he said. "Mama's in the kitchen making lunch. Your papa's going to change you, put you in a nice, dry diaper. Ginger—" he called out the open door. "The baby's wet. I'll do it."

Asher opened his mouth.

"Now, this is how we change a diaper," Kleinman said, picking him up. "We set you on the changing table. Oh, isn't that nice and soft. Nice, soft purple velvet underneath you. Now your papa has to find a diaper. Papa has to look for one." He called out to the kitchen, "Ginger, where did I put the diapers? Jimmy's wet." Softly, he said, "Papa's going to look in the dresser. Well, they're not in here. Isn't that funny that Papa can't remember where they are." Jimmy had shown him a box of them; he knew that. He had shown him where the wiping cloths were also, down low somewhere, underneath something. "Papa's going to look in the cabinet. No, they're not here, either. Hey, Ginger! Oh, that's right, Papa remembers. They're in the closet—Christ!"

Claudine was standing in the doorway.

"I'm sorry," she said. "I forgot my scarf."

"Jesus—"

"I should have knocked—"

"You must think I'm pathetic."

"I think you're beautiful. I'm going right now. I think you're unbelievably sweet. I wish I hadn't come back. But it was cold and I needed a scarf. But you just keep doing what you're doing. I think you're beautiful, a beautiful grandpa." She moved quickly toward him, hugged him, then backed out the door. "Just keep up what you're doing. Asher is lucky to have you. And you should be here all the time. Now I'm going."

Stop the car!" Kleinman said to the driver. "I want to get out right here."

"Here?"

"That's Lake Ashi, isn't it?"

"Guest cannot stop here. Nothing for see." The driver said something in Japanese to the guide, then turned around and smiled at Kleinman. "Resting room up a road," he said.

"No, I don't need a rest room. I just want to stop and look." He pretended to take out a camera and shoot pictures from the window. Below them, between two ridges, a silver crescent flashed among the trees. "The lake," he said. "That's Lake Ashi, isn't it?"

"Remains long time to Sounzan," said the guide.

"If it was sunny out we'd see Mount Fuji now, wouldn't we?"

"Mount Fuji almost always invisible."

"Yes, I know. But we're near, aren't we?"

The guide pointed to clouds on the far side of the depression that held the lake. "Still long time."

"That's okay. I just want to take a picture of the lake."

"We buy pictures later," said the guide. "Cute pictures of Mount Fuji and the lake. All on picture."

"Resting room up a road," said the driver.

They were not going very fast; the asphalt wound steeply uphill and they were on a tight curve. Kleinman opened the door and nearly fell out; the driver swerved onto the shoulder.

"Mr. Klein!" said the guide.

"Come on, honey!" he said, and he grabbed her arm and pulled her out with him. She was giggling again. He tugged her elbow, helped her along behind him as they headed down the shoulder to a break in the trees. It was fifty yards back. He could see the driver watching them in the side-view mirror. "There," Kleinman said, pointing, when they reached the view. "I knew it." In the corner of the inlet, which perfectly reflected the low, silvery clouds, a steep river had cut a ravine through the trees; in places it whitened— waterfalls plummeting from the steep-hewn escarpments. "Mount Fuji is that way, isn't it?" he said, pointing. "Right there, behind the river."

"Yes, yes," said the guide. "But today hidden. We buy cute picture up the road."

Kleinman bent down, started digging with his fingers. The ground was firm, a reddish pack like the soil in the Allegheny Mountains. It struck him, the similarity of the earth; he could be in western Pennsylvania. This is where his enemy lived.

The guide giggled. "What are Mr. Klein doing?"

"Planting tulips," he said, and he took the sack of bulbs from the pocket of his coat.

One day leaving his cello lesson, his gaze wandered into the cramped alcove of his teacher's kitchen, where on the table he saw a ring of medicine bottles, seven or eight of them, and a multitude of pills that lay in sorted piles around a compartmented plate. He turned his head away, but he saw his teacher's mood darken. Kleinman excused himself and opened the door, but the teacher said, "That's not a real Peccatte bow, you know."

"You're mistaken."

"I'm not mistaken. Believe me. That's a copy."

"It's not a copy. My father had a copy made, but I sold it to come to the States. I kept the original."

"No you didn't," his teacher said. "You kept the copy."

Kleinman went to a dealer in Haverhill, who confirmed by examining the varnish that the bow was a fake, no more than seventy-five years old. Kleinman had a good laugh at that, thinking of the dealer in Bristol whom he thought he had cheated. He had been just a boy then, but after living under his father's dark gaze, the transaction had given him the first sense of worldliness in his life. Ha! It was the dealer who had cheated *him*. What could he have expected? Children that age in the United States could barely buy candy at the store. Then, stepping off the T on his way back home, he realized his father had probably made two copies of the bow and cheated them both. This only made him laugh harder. The only part that saddened him was that he couldn't tell his wife.

He was reading in the kitchen when Asher started wailing. He had been perfectly content before then, upstairs in his crib, had actually fallen asleep as Kleinman watched—the tiny lids drawing suddenly closed. But now the sound came through the monitor like a siren. Then it stopped. Kleinman stood, pulled open the refrigerator, and surveyed his choices: a plate of cold noodles, some wilted asparagus in a bowl. It was ten-fifteen. Claudine and Jimmy had been at services half an hour: he had two more to go. Silence still. He chose the asparagus. Out the window, a woman in a long sweater was sweeping off the porch next door while peering in at him. She waved and he waved back, gave her the okay sign with his hand, then moved from the window. This must be Mrs. Diamond; that was comforting. He sat down with the bowl of asparagus and ate three stalks. The wailing started again.

He brought the asparagus upstairs with him to the nursery. Asher stared up at him, his face wrinkled in terror. Kleinman put down the bowl and stared back. He tried to smile but he knew the gesture was false, a shark's disguise. He gave up. His entire life he had been conscious of his menacing features—the hawkish nose, the hairless crown, the dark brow. This was not his fault, but it was undeniable. Children had always been wary of him; they had always run to Ginger. "Coochee-coo," he said. The same features had been an undeniable boon in business.

More cries.

"Your mom and pop will be home in two hours. No time at all. Grandpa Augie is here with you." He tilted his head to the side, stuck out his tongue. The shrieking ratcheted to a new pitch. "Okay, let's see—" He pulled a piece of asparagus from the bowl, waved it like a baton, then ate it. Asher quieted. Kleinman wasn't sure whether the baby was even watching, exactly—the eyes didn't seem to track—but a sudden calm deepened his features. Kleinman repeated the trick with another stalk. Abruptly, the wailing again.

Kleinman turned. In the corner, a basket of toys: a bear, a pile of rattles, some balls on a string. He picked up the bear, held it over the crib. He tried the rattles. A pause, then more shrieking. He looked at his watch: ten-twenty. He reached in, slid his hands underneath, and lifted him. Now the shrieks quieted, although he suspected that this only represented deepening fear. Asher stared, flat-eyed, like a fish on deck. Kleinman tossed him gently—once, twice—and pulled him to his chest. The shrieking started again.

They walked through the house. Kleinman showed him vases, windows, pictures, carpets, the knobs on the banisters and the glowing light switches on the walls, the tasseled cotton ornaments on the lampshades. The shrieking continued unabated through the kitchen, the hallway, the living room, the staircase, Jimmy and Claudine's bedroom, the living room again, the kitchen, the staircase, the nursery. It stopped for a moment when Kleinman examined the flat green night-light, but then began again immediately. Finally he opened the front door and stepped onto the porch. Suddenly Asher quieted, and when Kleinman propped him on in his forearm, he seemed to scan the view of the block. "That's a boy," Kleinman said. "That's a brave boy."

The air was cold and after a few minutes he turned and brought the baby back inside, but as soon as they were through the door again, the shrieking began once more, even louder. He walked back out and it stopped. He brought him inside to the hallway, struggled into his own jacket while the shrieking continued, then searched in the nursery for a coat for Asher; he managed to get the baby's arms into it while the cries tore at him; then they reemerged together onto the porch. Asher was instantly calm again, peering vaguely up the block. For a while, Kleinman moved back and forth from one foot to the other. Then he pulled his scarf from his pocket and wrapped it around Asher's neck. He set off down the front steps and up the street.

So there was a flu around: he would be careful. Two corners up, hidden behind a hill, he found a park. Asher was still quiet. As he crossed into the entrance, he realized he should have left a note for Claudine; but it was only ten-thirty and he had till noon, at least. He pulled the zipper up to Asher's chin and started across the expanse of new grass toward where he could see a children's playground on the other side of a soccer field. There he found a swing set, a slide, and a set of monkey bars. There was a woman there, Latin, watching a blond toddler dig in the sandbox. Kleinman went to the swings. He checked Asher's hands—warm as toast. The woman eyed him. He thought of Isabela. There were three swings of the regular kind and three others that, he could see, were designed for babies, with a metal bar that circled the seat. He lifted Asher over one of them and set him inside, pulled his legs through the slots, and gave the swing a tiny push. The woman darted over next to him. Asher's mouth opened.

"Excuse me," the woman said. "Do you really put that baby in the swing?"

"What did it look like I was doing?"

"How old is he? He is a boy?"

"Yes. Three months."

"He cannot hold his head yet."

"Then what's he doing?" Kleinman said. "Look." Asher was a ball of yellow cloth with a mouth in a joyful O.

The woman made a clicking noise with her tongue and moved off. Kleinman's ire surged. He pushed the swing a little harder. Asher was smiling now, his mouth wide open. Kleinman pushed the swing again and glanced toward the woman, who turned away and gathered her toddler from the sandbox. The boy began to cry and struggle, and the woman strode away across the park yanking him by the hand. Kleinman turned back to Asher and made funny faces at him while the swing slowed. Then he stopped pushing and waited until it stopped. He pulled him out and held him to his chest. Asher was calm again, still warm, and there was something undeniably trusting now in the way he buried himself in Kleinman's coat. The pull of blood, Kleinman thought.

At the street exit, he said, "Listen, Asher. Let Grandpa Augie be the first to tell you: Take the advice of no one."

A rapid descent. Or so it seemed to him. Though by the calendar it was the normal course of the disease. They'd gone to Barbados in the summer of '92. By the summer of '93, she'd grown quieter. By daylight, this was the only manifestation—the absence of her garrulousness. At the supermarket she no longer conversed with the butcher in her faint Boston accent, admonishing him to pick out the plumpest chicken from behind the glass; now she merely stood in front of the display, pointing. Kleinman went with her. He left the brewery at lunch every other day and took her shopping. In the produce aisle, she pointed and Kleinman gathered. Peaches. Apples. Strawberries. She no longer said the words, and at times he wasn't sure she knew them. Yet otherwise she was fine. He didn't want to test her. When they met friends, she could carry on a short social conversation as long as it didn't involve naming things or telling a story about what they'd done the week before. Once she told the Learys they'd spent February in St. Bart's. Where had this come from? Perhaps from Barbados the year before? Kleinman shifted nervously but revealed nothing; soon he learned to answer these questions himself. He watched the reactions of others. At a cocktail party she wore her alabaster brooch on her pants leg; Kleinman moved it, but later he saw it there again. At another party, he came out back to find her squatting in the host's shrubbery. So he stopped taking her to parties. But she still smiled. She still gardened. She still made dinner: roasts and fish from the expensive market. One evening there was a scarf in a casserole and the next day he hired a cook.

By the summer of '94 it was far worse. He noticed a pattern, the sun going down, the shadows approaching and then covering the house, the hour of the wolf descending. One evening in the bedroom he found her curled in a ball beneath their bed. "Ginger! Ginger! What are you doing! Come out to Augie!" A month later the bathroom window was open and she was lying outdoors on the steep gable roof in her nightgown. "My love! My love! Don't move! Augie is coming up to get you!" He had bolts installed on the windows. The neurologist suggested a chronic-care hospital, but he refused; instead, he hired a woman to help full time.

Her name was Rosa, a Guatemalan nearly Ginger's own age,

scoliotic but as spry as a squirrel. She charged around the house, bent at the waist, scrubbing floors and cleaning up after meals; followed Ginger on her walks; ironed Kleinman's shirts with lemon in the water; clipped the hedges. Kleinman paid her extravagantly. This was money the abomination, but he was going to use it now! Curse the wretched mistake of his life! Rosa followed Ginger everywhere she went, sat in the dirt next to her while she planted bulbs, dug them, planted them again. She was infinitely patient and as watchful as a baby nurse, and Kleinman paid her twice the going rate. He planned to raise it to three times once she'd shown her commitment. He himself cut down to half days at the brewery and gave over his responsibilities to the new hire. He spent his afternoons shopping with the two of them and helping with the work of the household. He would have quit the brewery completely, but in truth work was a relief. At home Ginger still performed the physical tasks but was completely silent now and withdrew at sundown like an animal of the forest. He rid the house of its lawn and planted flowers all the way across their property, because she liked to tend them, Rosa at her side. The sunflowers rose taller than their heads and together they walked between them, holding hands like lovers. Ginger was upright; Rosa was stooped—the irony. Kleinman walked behind. He put on music in the evenings to get them through the particular hour of her dread, the shadows climbing from the lawn to the high windows; and he hired a dance teacher to come to the house every evening at six. When fall came, he moved the appointment to five. The teacher was an enthusiastic homosexual man named Ray DiGranza, who took Ginger in his arms and twirled her, to her surprised delight.

Kleinman teamed with Rosa and they learned the waltz and the fox-trot, Kleinman holding her across her inclined back. To his utter surprise, Ginger could still learn something new—as long as Ray DiGranza was leading. She was silent as they danced, but as Ray DiGranza turned and dipped her around the living room, he could see in her eyes a fierce concentration that he chose to read, because he did not want to imagine the alternative, as pleasure.

That winter he hired another woman, Mrs. Fielding, a registered nurse, and now there were four people in the house. Kleinman slept down the hall in Hannah's room and Ginger slept alone in their bed. Sometime that year she had become afraid of him at night, had failed to recognize him under the covers beside her. But by day she was better. In a cot alongside her bed was Rosa, and in Jimmy's old room was Mrs. Fielding, a buzzer rigged to wake her.

One night that winter he woke in Hannah's room and could not fall back asleep. He walked down the hall and peeked in at Ginger in their bedroom, snoring evenly, and at Rosa in the cot by the door. He walked back to Hannah's room, switched on the light, and sat at her desk. It was a child's desk, he realized suddenly. How had he not seen that? Hadn't it bothered Hannah when she was a teenager? It occurred to him that he had never truly imagined his children's lives. He moved to the rocker by the window, covered in chintz. Hannah had been an enthusiastic child. So had her brother Harry, but enthusiastic in a different manner. Harry climbed trees and talked about flying airplanes and jumped off the high rocks into the water at the quarry. Hannah's enthusiasm, on the other hand, had always been social. An eagerness, really. When they went to the beach at Atlantic City, it was Hannah who always rose from the sand and went out into the water to swim with him, to dangle by her legs as he carried her out through the spraying surf. Harry and Jimmy had never done that. Kleinman would tread water, holding up his daughter as she floated on her back, and tell her stories about the brewery as the swells lifted and dropped them together. She'd been that way all through high school, never a rebellion, never the cigarettes that he'd found in the toes of Jimmy's school shoes or the package of condoms that had dropped one morning from the lining of one of Harry's ties.

He sat upright in the tiny desk chair and switched on the light above her shelves. The entire room still looked juvenile. A framed portrait of a stallion by the door. Two large stuffed rabbits on the windowsill. Her trigonometry and civics texts were lined up on the shelves, but next to them was a set of books that she must last have read in the fourth grade. Was she trying to tell him something? Had he not wanted her to grow up? He recalled her child's voice, the determined quietness of her enthusiasm for him, the scrabble of her slippery feet on his thighs as he pushed her through the breaking surf: three children gone. An insistent distance where once he had taken for granted their resolute claims for his affection. On the phone now Harry talked about his progress toward the instrument rating on his aviation license. Jimmy was brief with him, the remnant of his sullenness from long in the past; in truth, he preferred getting Claudine on the line. Hannah remained his daughter, but she was in Northern California, which seemed to be a culture all to itself. She was still single and had never felt comfortable telling him about her boyfriends. He picked up one of her books, *The Runaway Mare of Seaside City*, and glanced through the pages.

When he looked up, Ginger was at the door in her night-clothes.

"I was just looking at some of our daughter Hannah's things," he said. He made a habit of talking to her now, of telling her everything he was doing. It was the way she herself used to speak to the children, a habit Kleinman had admired wonderingly when the boys were small. "Mommy's making toast," she used to say. "First Mommy puts the bread in the toaster, then Mommy sets down the toasted bread and butters it—" Kleinman had always envied her patience, her natural instincts with children. Now he found it easy to replicate them. In the interim, some internal drive had wound down inside of him, leaving patience. "I was looking at some of our daughter Hannah's books," he said. "Look at this. Hannah still has her baby books on the shelves."

Ginger entered the room and sat on the bed. Rosa appeared in the doorway, looking sleepy, and Kleinman gestured her back to her room.

"This is the story of the runaway mare of Seaside City," Kleinman said.

Ginger lay back on Hannah's pillows and stared dreamily at the ceiling. " 'In a house by the sea, in a town on a curve, lived a mare and a colt, and the man that they served.' " Kleinman wiped his eyes. " 'Of the names that one heard, in this town on a curve, were the strangest and longest and oddest of terms.' " He ran his fingers back and forth on her hair. At one point, when the mare leapt the hedges and ran into the sea, Ginger raised her legs and actually scissored them above her, the very gesture Hannah used to make when he used to read her these lines before bed.

~~~~~~~~~~~~~~~~~~~~~~~~~~~~~~~~~~

By the time he heard Claudine and Jimmy's car, Asher was asleep in his lap on the rocking chair: Kleinman had been sitting motionless for forty-five minutes. His shoulders ached and his forearm was damp with moisture from the baby's head. He was holding a bottle, but Asher hadn't taken it. Finally, he heard the garage opener; an instant later Claudine was in the door, then Jimmy.

"Shhh," she said.

"Good work, Pop."

"We're friends now," Kleinman said, "your boy and me."

"How was he?"

"An angel."

Claudine disappeared back into the garage.

"Really?" Jimmy said.

"A devil at first. But now an angel. He's a real athlete, your son."

"He is?" Jimmy looked pleased.

"Excellent balance. An acrobat."

"What did you two do?"

"Just played around. Nothing big."

Claudine appeared again. "Did he need to be changed?" she asked.

"Oops—" Kleinman said. "Oh well, I guess I forgot. I mean, I guess I didn't realize—well, he was upset at the start. I had to distract him."

Claudine laughed. "It's been a long time."

"Since ten," said Kleinman.

"I mean, since you had a baby around."

While Kleinman sat with Asher, Claudine and Jimmy went upstairs. Kleinman shifted his weight finally for comfort and Asher stirred, opened his dark eyes for a moment, then closed them again. From upstairs, Kleinman heard the shut of drawers, the clink of hangers, intermittent bits of low conversation. He listened for his own name but didn't hear it. Claudine's voice was brighter than Jimmy's, sharper, and Jimmy's in reply was low and abrupt, a resigned quality to the short words. This had never changed. As a boy, Harry had possessed an ease with talk that Jimmy, the middle child, had failed to gain, even after decades. This, in Kleinman's mind, had led to the religion, years later— Harry was an atheist, and in truth something of a rogue. And somehow Jimmy had ended up with a sense of misfortune from this, of ill luck in comparison to his brother. A boy never overcame that, it seemed, the slights absorbed in elementary school. From misfortune to religion—a small step.

On the stairs, the talk resumed. Jimmy and Claudine's marriage was like a friendship, it seemed to Kleinman, two boats on a calm bay. His own with Ginger had been of a different sort; there had been passion—perhaps not all the way to the end, but for a good part of their years—as well as all that it had brought. In fifty years she'd left him twice, once in Atlantic City on a trip they'd taken on their first anniversary, when she disappeared from the hotel lobby one evening and stayed away two nights while Kleinman strolled defiantly along the wintry beaches. She called him each evening but would not explain, and on the third day she returned. He'd taken her back immediately, no thought of otherwise, and though he suspected it was her family—she had uncles in New Jersey—he understood the conceivable consequences of inquiry and allowed himself no questions. This was the price of their ardor. And over the years—a great miracle—it had never soured, only occasionally inverted to a brief, stinging anger that necessitated certain expression. Yet all in all, a great blessing for which to be eternally thankful. A sweet and salty life. The second time she left was right after Jimmy was born—two children in the house now, and one afternoon Ginger simply walked away. She called from the post office a mile from the house, said she was on a walk and would be back the next morning. Kleinman remembered the feeling, looking up from the phone: Jimmy swaddled on the tabletop; Harry balancing upright on a tricycle in the living room. She had merely meant to show him how deeply important she was, he realized later, how fundamentally necessary to their survival; she could have returned after that single moment on the phone and Kleinman would never have forgotten the point. But she managed to stay away past nightfall anyway, returning at last to find him asleep in the rocker with Jimmy in his arms and Harry laid out flat on the carpeted floor at his feet. He remembered looking up and seeing her in the doorway, the feeling of relief. Without Ginger, he'd realized at that moment, he was a stranger to his own life.

Perhaps that is why Jimmy had chosen this, four decades

later—a marriage of imperturbable calm. He and Claudine still seemed polite with each other, somehow, after eight years and a child. He noticed the way Jimmy jumped up to bring the butter to the table, to serve the vegetables, to clear the plates for dessert. And when Asher needed changing, it was Jimmy who did it— eagerly, it seemed to Kleinman, like a boy making up for misbehavior. After a few minutes of listening to their sparse conversation upstairs, Kleinman shifted in the chair and Asher woke again, perplexed. He stared up at his grandfather, not crying yet, not afraid, but clearly puzzled—and Kleinman wondered if he was having the first inkling of the bafflement of life. His father's face but different, etched by time, inexplicably closer to passing, staring down at him. Then, after a moment, the crying.

Jimmy clomped down the stairs. He picked up Asher, carried him to the changing room making O's with his mouth and a popping noise that drew the baby's attention immediately. Kleinman followed, waited to see if Asher would look back at him for verification of the riddle of life, waited to see if he was right about the human soul. But he wasn't. Asher, in his father's hands, quieted and was content at the broad, popping lips.

Jimmy said, "I'll do one more diaper. You watch. Then I'll watch you do the next one."

"You already showed me everything."

"And do you remember it all?"

"No."

"Then watch, Pop."

In fact, Kleinman had to admire his son for what he did next. The sureness of the hands. The expressive face, leaning over the table, still popping his lips to distract Asher as he pulled off the old diaper and slid on the new. The swift closure and rebundling. Jimmy stood. Asher was smiling, scissoring his tiny legs. Jimmy hoisted him onto one shoulder and carried him out to the living room, where Claudine said, "Thank you, sweetheart," and kissed him on the cheek.

Jimmy said, "Pop thinks Asher is going to be a good athlete."

"He'll walk early," Claudine said. "Look at those legs. My sister's boy walked at ten months."

"So did Harry," Kleinman said. "Jimmy's brother—actually, he walked at nine months."

"That's extraordinarily early," said Claudine.

"Claudine already knows that," Jimmy said. "You didn't take Asher outside, did you?"

"Pardon?"

"I noticed his coat was out when we got back. I asked you not to take him outside."

"Oh, that's fine," said Claudine.

"No it's not. Not if we asked him not to."

"Jimmy, it's your father, sweetheart. He's careful with him."

"Did you take Asher outside?"

"Yes, I did."

"I thought you said you didn't."

"Well, now I'm saying I did. I wasn't specifically asked."

"Where?"

"To the park."

Jimmy turned his back, walked to the window.

"Sweetheart, it's nothing," said Claudine.

"He was terrific," Kleinman said. "He adored it."

"It's not nothing. What did you do? I thought you said you were at home."

"We just walked."

"Well, I'm asking you not to in the future."

"Not to walk with his grandson?"

"Not to do what we ask him not to."

"All right," Kleinman said. "All right."

Claudine said, "Jimmy, your father is doing us a wonderful favor to baby-sit. He can do whatever he wants. What is the matter with you?"

"Nothing's the matter with me," said Jimmy. "What's the matter with everyone else?"

⸻⸻⸻⸻⸻⸻⸻⸻

W hen they reached the town, Kleinman told the guide that he knew only the first name of the woman he was coming to see but that her age, more or less, would be near to his. She laughed at this, the bee again, flying out between her fingers. But then she commented that Umi, at least, was not a common name and that Sounzan was a tiny hamlet: perhaps she could be of help. They had ridden a steep funicular to reach the village, and now, on a central avenue, she had Kleinman wait in the hired car while she inquired in a tea shop. The road was rimmed by low post-and-beam structures whose functions Kleinman could not discern; the guide emerged from the tea shop, crossed the street, and entered another building, which looked to be a restaurant or perhaps a small grocery. When she appeared again and returned to the car, she laughed quickly and told him that she had found the family he was looking for.

Kleinman fingered the portfolio. Their driver brought them a short distance up a steep, overgrown hill to a house near the summit, shaded in tall pines; it was built of wood and stucco, low to the street, spanned at its roof by a concave Oriental arch that rested on posts midway along its upswept tails. On the way up the walk, Kleinman's courage began to fail, but then the door opened and a man appeared, bowing. The guide spoke, and when she was finished, the man smiled and handed Kleinman a business card, bowing again. One side was in Japanese, but the other was in English:

Teiji Yamamoto
Overseas Representative, London Office
Bank of Japan

The guide interpreted as Kleinman explained that he was here for an unusual reason—he paused, and bowed slightly himself, steadying the portfolio under his arm. In his possession was a document that belonged, if he was not mistaken, to the man's mother. He waited a moment after each phrase so that the guide could translate; but when she had finished, Teiji Yamamoto turned to Kleinman and thanked him in English. He bowed again, then invited them all into the garden.

Out back, they walked to a grove of purple plums bordering an

expanse of steep slope—Sounzan was not crowded like Tokyo.
There, after the exchange of a further round of pleasantries, the
driver, who had followed them inside, photographed all of them
together in various combinations, standing and sitting. Then Teiji
Yamamoto led Kleinman to the rearmost glade on the property,
walled in by a line of firs, where he stopped beside a polished
stone of red-hued marble, set in the earth on a hill amid clusters of
brilliantly leafed shrubs, it was the size and shape of a large egg-
plant. Teiji Yamamoto was speaking in English, but in Kleinman's
state—he was fatigued from travel and mildly dizzy from
hunger—the accent made the words nearly unintelligible. Soon,
he lost altogether the sense of what was being said. He found himself nodding politely. His host gestured again at the polished
stone, and though it was rather dull amid the profusion of autumn
color, Kleinman understood that he was being asked to say something. He began to compliment it, out of courtesy, when suddenly
he realized that it was Umi Yamamoto's memorial. He fell silent.
In an improvised gesture, he closed his eyes, bowed deeply, then
clapped twice as he stood. This seemed to please his host, who
bowed again in return. He led Kleinman back across the garden,
gesturing kindly at obstacles along the stone walk, the way Ginger
used to do.

At the door of the house, a Caucasian woman was waiting for
them. She turned out to be Teiji Yamamoto's wife, Claire, and
after Teiji introduced her, he excused himself and disappeared inside. Kleinman was shaken. What was he to do now? Why had he
assumed that Umi Yamamoto would still be alive? In front of him
was an English-speaking woman with a pleasantly forward de-

meanor, but she seemed to be, he guessed, only about Jimmy's age; an old protectiveness reared inside him. Perhaps he had erred in the entire endeavor. What could he say to a person tied only remotely to these events? What could he say to Teiji, even, most of a lifetime later? He struggled for words, leaning against the doorpost because his balance seemed thickened. Claire Yamamoto reached for his arm and led him onto a patio along the side wall of the house, where she gestured to two chairs of woven yellow cane standing in the shade. Her hair was Asiatic, and in her eyes was a mild epicanthic suggestion of the East; but her skin was olive, and her nose, which Kleinman saw in profile as they took their seats, was bent gently downward at its peak. At this he smiled: Semitic? Could she be a Jew? The Diaspora seed, cast like windfall across the earth? There was an obvious sympathy to her demeanor for which he was suddenly and childishly grateful. He grinned at her, settling himself into the chair. She smiled in return. Then, without preamble, she explained to him that she and Teiji had lived in Sounzan all last year caring for Umi, who had died six months ago, in this house, of old age.

"I'm very sorry," said Kleinman.

"Thank you for your concern."

"*Dayan haemet*—" Kleinman said.

She smiled slightly.

"It's what we say," he said. "You know—upon learning that someone's passed away." He found himself taking hold of the lapels of his jacket and realized, looking down at his vitiligo-paled hands, that this was a memory of his stepfather half a century before: at the radio announcement of the death of the Zionist

Nahum Sokolow, Hank Kleinman had reached down without hesitation and ripped the pocket off his own shirtfront. "The Jews, I mean," Kleinman said. "It's what they say: *dayan haemet.* And they rend their garments. We rend our garments." He paused, considered the possibility that he might have been wrong about her. "Just superstitions," he said. "To tear what is over your heart. Something from my stepfather's generation. I'm sorry to ramble like this." He clasped his hands. "Primitives—all of us."

Claire Yamamoto looked back toward the house. "After Umi passed away," she said, "we returned to London, for Teiji's job." Her accent was British. She leaned toward him now, her features darkened. "But now once again we've come back here. This time it's to care for Teiji's father, in there. Or at least make arrangements for him. He is also, unfortunately, quite ill." She pointed with her chin through a screen toward a back room, in which Kleinman suddenly saw a dark figure stirring on a mat.

"Again, I'm sorry."

"Don't be."

"You and your husband are very kind."

She turned abruptly, leaned toward him, and said, "Kakuzo is horrible to Teiji."

Kleinman looked around. Teiji was still inside the house, and the guide stood with the driver at a distance out in the garden, apparently intimidated by the English conversation. "He has never treated him like his brothers. Never encouraged him in his work," she continued in a voice that seemed too loud for the arrangement. "And now he takes it as his due that we come back from London to take care of him. I don't know how much longer I can take it." She gestured at the window, where Kleinman saw that the old man was now sitting next to the screen.

"I'm very sorry," he said. "I know how that is."

"Do you?"

"Yes, I do. I have lost someone myself. And, I might add, I am also a father." He lowered his voice. "May I ask you—what work of Teiji's is not encouraged?"

"Oh, it doesn't matter."

"Yes it does."

"Well then," said Claire Yamamoto. "It's his painting. Teiji is a beautiful painter, if you want to know. But because of his father he is working at Bank of Japan. It's rather difficult for a man like Teiji. It's what's expected of him here." She paused. "But the point is we're not here anymore—we're in London now. Teiji could do as he pleases. He's not a typical Japanese man. I mean, look—he's in there fixing us something to eat. And he's the one who looks after his father. His brothers don't. But he does. He's unusual—too good a man if you ask me. But we don't have to do it the way Kakuzo wants. We could live jolly well on less. My father always dreamed of being a tenor, but he managed a pharmacy instead. Forgive me, but that pharmacy killed him. There's a lesson in that for all of us. Money isn't everything. I want Teiji to do what he loves, to follow his art. But his father"—she gestured at the window, where the old man seemed to nod his head slightly at Kleinman—"his father owns a tatami shop. Do you know what tatami are? They're mats. For the floor. They're floor mats. For Kakuzo, the only thing more grand than floor mats is a big bank. He wouldn't know art if it bit him on the bum." Kleinman saw her compose herself. "But look at me," she said. "I'm the one who's rambling on. Tell me again what brings you here to Sounzan."

"I had something for your husband's mother," Kleinman said. "A letter."

"How did you know Umi?"

"I didn't. The letter isn't from me."

"Ah—who's it from, then?"

Kleinman said, "Excuse me, you said your husband is a painter?"

"A wonderful one," she said.

"Was Umi an artist also?"

"No. She was a lovely woman. Very gentle. Very accepting of me. But never an artist."

"And Kakuzo is not, either."

She glanced at the window, chuckling. "Certainly not," she said, rising. "Here—let me show you some of Teiji's work. The house is full of it, though his father won't hang it. Can you imagine?" She glared in the direction of the old man, who seemed not to notice. Then she led Kleinman from the patio into a toolshed off the garden, where she pulled back a dusty tarp to reveal a stack of watercolors reaching halfway up the wall. Kleinman sorted through them, pulling them out from the pile. They were landscapes, rivers beneath mountains, variegated sunlight in tree leaves: quite excellent to his eye—a dark and confident hand. "Yes," he said. "I see what you mean—quite lovely. Thank you for showing me."

"Not at all. I agree with you completely. They are rather exquisite if you ask me. He could have a career in London. I'm going to take these back with us and show them around. Teiji laughs when I tell him that, because Kakuzo has convinced him that they're worthless." She shook her head. "You can't undo that."

"Yes, I know," he answered. There was a silence in which fleetingly he thought of Jimmy standing against the living room wall as the other children entered the house for a birthday party. "Tell me," Kleinman whispered. "Were his parents—Teiji's father, there, in the other room—was he happily married to Mrs. Yamamoto?"

"Whatever could you mean?"

"Forgive me for intruding."

She looked at him closely. "May I ask who the letter is from?"

"I think it's from Teiji's father," he answered. Then, more softly, "His real father, I mean. You see, I was in the war. A soldier's effects came into my possession. A soldier in the Japanese army. I believe he might have been your husband's father."

"I don't understand—"

"His true father."

She turned sideways to him, her gaze lowered. Again there was the tentative recognition for Kleinman of his own blood, but now there was clearly something Japanese in her posture as well, a repentant tilt to her head. The Japanese, he knew, made elaborate shows of apology. It never seemed quite necessary to him; yet now it seemed crushingly so.

"I think I was the one who killed your husband's father."

"I don't understand."

"Perhaps you will when you read the letter. I'd like to give it to you, though it ought to go to your husband. I have a feeling he'll find it important." He thought of his own mother sitting down across from him in the flat on Beach 28th Street with an envelope in her hand. "Liberating even—perhaps. But I think it would be better for you to read it to him. That's what I think. It's quite a serious piece of news."

"What?" she said, and when she looked up, he saw that the blood had drained from her face. Yet it was she who spoke. "Dear God," she said, stepping across the small shed with her hand out toward him. "Are you all right?"

~~~~~~~~~~~~~~~~~~~~

While Jimmy and Claudine prepared dinner to break the fast, Kleinman went upstairs to change Asher. He had wanted to change him, had asked to do it, now that he felt at ease. It was a ritual of such sweetness: the baby's creased little eyes, smiling; the corpulent hands; the tiny, pliant limbs. Asher was on the changing table, and Kleinman was looking for the wipes again. They were supposed to be in the cabinet. That's what had happened lately: people had to tell him things twice. He was feeling a little faint. At Bread & Circus recently he'd forgotten where the aprons hung. The green aprons he put on every day. It was a question of automatic pilot. Things he did without thinking. Think about them and they blow away like smoke. Asher looked patient enough, his head turned to watch Kleinman across the room. The wipes were not in the cabinet. They were not in the toy trunk. They were not on the closet shelf.

The sound of a dropped melon. He wheeled. Jimmy on the floor next to the changing table. No, it was Asher. Please, Lord. He scooped him in his arms. Set him back on the platform. There. How did you fall? No, it wasn't blood—it was the red Onesie. There, my sweetest angel. It's only the Onesie. And only three feet down onto carpet. Not even three feet. Frantic crying now. That was a good sign. I have held a child draped in blood who made no sound. Oh my God. Here, my sweetie; here, my joy. Grandpa Augie is here. Here, my life. He turned Asher and examined him. Already a bump on the back of the skull. Impossibly fast. At the crown of the occiput. Oh, my sweetest. Oh, my treasure. He carried him into the bedroom, to the light of the window. "That's a baby." Bouncing him. "That's a baby. Look, there's a birdie in the tree. A big birdie in the tree." The bump was like bruised fruit. I will keep it from rising. "That's a baby," Kleinman said. "That's a baby. Now go to sleep."

Claudine was next to him.

"He fell," said Kleinman.

"I know," she said. "What did he hit?" She was panting. In her arms Asher quieted.

Then Jimmy was there. "Fuck! I told you!"

"Shhh," said Claudine.

"He fell onto the rug. I don't think it was bad. He has a little bump."

"He has a bump, honey. Fuck! It's exactly what I told you. Let me see it."

"He's fine," said Claudine. "Babies fall. Look. Aren't you? Aren't you fine?"

"He's going to Dr. Patton. Oh my God, look at the size of that."

"Oh, he's fine, honey. He gets one that big when he bumps the crib. Don't you? Did you have a little fall?"

"He's going to Dr. Patton. Fuck! Did you use the strap?"

But when Dr. Patton met them at the clinic, he said what Claudine had said. "He's fine. Babies fall." He took Asher in his arms, ushered the four of them straight back past the empty offices to an examining room, where he looked into his eyes with a penlight and pressed quickly on all his limbs with his facile, pediatrician's hands. By then Asher was playing with a cloth ring, holding it against his nose. "Doesn't look like he's too bothered," said Dr. Patton.

"And the bump?" said Jimmy.

"Children swell. It's what they're designed to do."

"My father was changing him," Jimmy said.

"And you should be glad of that—it's unusual enough." Dr. Patton nodded at Kleinman. "I'd just make sure he acts his usual self. Nurses normally. Naps normally."

"You're sure?" Jimmy said. "You're positive he's all right?"

"I can't be positive," the doctor said. "But I'm very confident."

"See?" Jimmy said to Claudine. "I told you." He turned Dr. Patton. "When I was little, he used to throw me, too," he said. "Quite high."

It was late October, and in the living room of the house in Newton Ray DiGranza was leading Ginger through half-turns of the East Coast Swing when suddenly on a pass by the side-yard window she was taken by an idea: it was time to plant the bulbs. "Winter, I forgot," she said, looking out at the blustery trees. "The tulips have to go into their beds."

The sky was clear and they were still a month from snow, but she seemed somehow impish to Kleinman at that moment, almost youthful in her step. He said, "Why not, if that's what you want."

Ray DiGranza said, "It's awfully cold out there."

"Oh, let's go, please!" Ginger said. "Let's plant them."

Ray DiGranza said, "I didn't bring a sweater."

But Kleinman said, "Beautiful. Beautiful. Everyone out to the yard."

"I'm a dance instructor."

"We'll dance then, too."

"Oh yes," said Ginger, taking Ray DiGranza's wrist—she might have thought he was a child.

In the chill wind out back, they both knelt next to her as she worked with the velvet sack of bulbs between her knees. At the base of the large sycamore, still holding Ray DiGranza's hand, she began digging with her fingers. Kleinman handed her a trowel, she let it drop. The ground was still soft around the trunk, mulched with stringy bark by the gardener, and she dug a hole and poured bulbs into it.

Ray DiGranza said, "Now cover it up."

She looked up, puzzled. "Santo," she said.

"Pardon?"

"Santo, what are you doing here?"

Kleinman said, "That's Ray DiGranza, your teacher. Remember, dear, one bulb per hole. Or they won't flower. You showed me that."

"Oh, ten bulbs in a hole is fine," Ray DiGranza said. "Now cover it up."

"You're home so early."

"They won't flower," said Kleinman. "Remember how you used to do it? In Pittsburgh?"

"Here," said Ray DiGranza. "I'll help you cover it." He knelt behind her, took both her hands in his own, and poured dirt over the hole. "Now, back inside to dance."

"Santo," she said. "This is August. There's no reason you two can't be friends. August has converted."

"What?" said Kleinman.

She rose clumsily, first to one knee, then to the other, then to her feet, and—some memory of the position they were in, Ray DiGranza behind, holding her hands—she began to turn slowly around as though exiting a twirl.

Ray DiGranza said, "Awfully cold for this, my dear, I would say. Come on, let's mosey on back inside."

But she continued the move haltingly and began to pull him toward the cedar fence. There was something in her eyes now, a glimmer of the drunkard's shining abandon, that Kleinman noted as she started across the grass underneath Ray DiGranza's outstretched arm. Then she unclasped herself from his fingers, turned slowly once more across the path of flagstones, and made her way in a failing three-beat dance step to the garden bench, where she reached her arms back like a barroom singer to prop herself on the handrail. "Oh, Augie," she said. Kleinman rose to his feet. "Something awful—" She went from the bench to the grass, managed to tilt her head up to find him for a moment—her eyes were pleading. Then they were vacant. He was crossing the yard when she fell. He lifted her, and her chest rose up like a body pulled from water. He went to his knees, reached up his fist, and brought it down on the spot where her sweater pushed upward at the sternum. She was limp in his arms. He punched again, felt the breastbone crack under the blow, and looked up to find Ray DiGranza cowering against the tree.

"Goddamn you to hell!" Kleinman shouted. "Call a doctor!" And he leaned his mouth down and pressed it onto hers.

~~~~~~~~~~~~~~~~~~

C ome on," said Jimmy. "We're all starving."

"It's not sundown yet," Claudine said. "Sundown is six twenty-one."

Kleinman looked at her.

"She gets the exact time from the paper," Jimmy said.

"I'm all right," said Kleinman. "I can wait."

"Did you eat, Pop?"

"Nothing at all. A real fast."

"I don't believe you," said Jimmy.

"Good, Grandpa Augie," said Claudine. "See, Jimmy? Your father obeys the rules."

"Pop, she's angry because I ate an apple this afternoon. I was getting dizzy."

"It's not such a good thing to obey all the rules," Kleinman said. "Believe me. And actually, Rabbi Becker would tell you the apple is fine. Better than fainting. That's Jewish law, Claudine."

"You're referring to *pikuakh nefesh*," said Claudine.

"Boy!" said Kleinman.

"Don't take her on, Pop. Believe me."

"Zeal of the convert," Claudine said.

Jimmy sat down on the couch. "Hey, I have a joke," he said. He cleared his throat. "All his life, a man tells his son, 'I don't care what you do, just don't marry a Gentile.' "

Kleinman had heard this one before, perhaps a variation. Jimmy had never been a good joke teller—in his mouth, the words were a chore. It was Harry who had inherited Kleinman's own ease with delivery. Odd that this was how you got to be provost, that this was how you got to run a brewery—just a little ease with words, with groups. That was all it was. He turned to listen to Jimmy. "This goes on for years," Jimmy said. "Finally, the son calls him one day and says, 'Guess what, Pop? I'm marrying a Gentile.' "

Here he paused. Kleinman looked around.

"Anyway—the father is heartbroken." Jimmy glanced at his watch. It was the wrong time to hesitate in the delivery. "The son says, 'But don't worry, she's converting.' " Another glance at his watch. "Okay," he said. "The father thinks this is a little better. So the woman converts to being a Jew. They get married, and over the years the father finally begins to accept her." He rubbed his hands together, swallowed. Kleinman could see him getting nervous—this is what killed the jokes. "Then, one Friday night, the father calls the son and the wife and invites them over for dinner. But the wife says, 'Hold on, it's Friday night. We can't drive the car over there. It's the Sabbath!' " A glance out the window. He was organizing the punch line—Kleinman could see his mind working. Then he spoke triumphantly. " 'See,' the father says to the son. 'I told you—you shouldn't have married a Gentile!' "

Claudine burst out laughing.

Kleinman laughed too, trying to encourage Jimmy. He was seventy-eight years old; Jimmy was almost fifty. He thought of his wife: Ginger would have noticed his effort, would have thanked him later in the car.

"Pop, what's the matter?"

Finally, he said, "Hey, what smells so delicious?"

~~~~~~~~~~~~~~~~~~~~~~~~

One day coming out the door of his condominium in the Back Bay, Kleinman heard the mailman speaking in German from the downstairs letter boxes, and another memory came to him: his mother prevailing in an argument with his father in the atrium of the Hamburg house while, from upstairs on the landing, he listened, as he always did, for evidence of his father's affection; a vitreous light flickering on the walls from the ceaseless waves on the canal; his mother insisting that he spend more time at his studies while his father, the bilious capitalist who had wept openly the evening before upon hearing Emanuel Feuermann play the Bach Second Suite, wanted him to start lessons on the cello.

And yet another, unsummoned, while passing Waterstone's Bookstore on Newbury Street in the Back Bay: a display of children's works in the window and a diorama, curiously painted, of a covered wagon among wild horses on the prairie, a river ambling alongside them. Propped against the diorama, the work of Laura Ingalls Wilder: *On the Banks of Plum Creek. Farmer Boy. By the Shores of Silver Lake.* On Hannah's shelf in Squirrel Hill a hardback copy of *Little House in the Big Woods* had sat, long after Hannah had gone, and Kleinman had taken to reading it to Ginger, near the end of her life, every morning and night. He had brought it north with them, purely out of nostalgia, when they moved to Boston. On the back porch in Newton, they would sit together in the sun and he would read aloud while Rosa prepared their breakfast; and in the evening, he would continue the story from a chair positioned near her bedroom door. She curled away from him, beneath the covers, smaller and smaller as the months progressed. He tried other books, but they bored them both, novels and history and even humor, which he read to her in a valiant voice. Yet he always returned to *Little House in the Big Woods.* There was something about the adventures of the pioneer girl in the cabin that kindled her concentration. Sometimes she would laugh, remembering some bit. Perhaps she had read it as a child. The thought occurred to him that she mistook her present situation—he knew he had the hawkish face of her father. That was all right with him. He had always felt that way toward her anyway, especially after Harry was born—that the real reason he was on earth was to guard her, her and her children, for as long as he lived.

~~~~~~~~~~~~~~~~~~~~~~~~~~~~~~

In the evening there was a note written in English on the door of Kleinman's guest-house quarters, and early the following morning, the guide, after rearranging Kleinman's train ticket, escorted him down the hill to a tea shop in town. When the car dropped them, she followed him across the cobblestone street to the door, where he had to explain to her that since there was no need for translation, he desired to do this alone. She giggled again—this was her reaction to every moment, he realized, that did not unfold effortlessly—but he could see now that there was also a new seriousness in her demeanor. He wondered what Claire Yamamoto had told her. He also wondered what Claire Yamamoto had told her husband. Might Teiji Yamamoto seek revenge?

To die in a tea shop on vacation in a hamlet in the hills of Japan: his rancor for the enemy had disappeared, but as he crossed the threshold of thick timbers into the dim shop, he again recalled his training at Camp Blanding. In the darkness, he stepped subtly against the wall, holding the burlap packet against his chest, and waited for his eyes to adjust. Two young men lounged in bamboo chairs at the rear, smoking hand-rolled cigarettes and playing

cards. They looked up at him, said something that sounded inso-
lent, and returned to their hands. Kleinman saw an open door behind them leading to a rear room with a patio.

There he found Teiji Yamamoto. At a small table behind a
spreading tree whose trunk hid half his body, he sat waiting for his
tea to steep, one hand beneath the slats of the bamboo bench.
From inside the teahouse, Kleinman circled wide so that he could
see the hidden hand, but when he realized it was empty, he
changed his route and approached so that Teiji Yamamoto would
notice him. He was aware still of the possibility of violence. The
table was empty except for a cup and a teapot, and there was
nothing nearby on the floor; Kleinman held the packet tightly
under his arm. What experience could prepare a man for this? He
remembered his own shattering news, also delivered late. But it
was not until he was next to the table that Teiji Yamamoto looked
up. He was trembling.

Kleinman had a sudden paternal hunch, and without pausing he
reached sideways across the table and hugged him quickly across
the shoulders; Teiji Yamamoto recoiled. Kleinman said, "Sorry—
maybe you don't do that here."

"No, no. That was quite all right." He seemed apologetic. "I
ordered your tea." He raised his hand to the boy behind the
counter, then looked down again into his lap.

Kleinman said, "This won't be easy."

"No. No." Teiji Yamamoto kept his eyes hidden, looking first at
the ground, then into his cup as he sipped from it.

"Did your wife tell you—"

"Yes," he said suddenly, looking up. He inhaled sharply. "What was my father like?"

Of course, of course—this is what he would want. Some news of the man, some clue. Not revenge. Of course not. Seventy years, his own children, and still the captious memory of his own father in Hamburg—the derisive note of his laughter. How could Kleinman have expected anything different? "Well," he said. "You see—we were in a theater of war."

Teiji Yamamoto continued to regard him expectantly. Kleinman's mind went to the cave on Aguni, but he felt nothing; the pictures moved before him unconvincingly, their centers lost. He saw the doorway of rock, the glimpse in bulb-light of a painted figure on the limestone; nothing more. The boy arrived with his tea. Kleinman sipped it. It was not yet steeped. In age, Teiji Yamamoto was near Jimmy and Harry. Kleinman said, "Your father spoke of you."

"Yes?"

"Before he passed away." He should have said *before he died.* But in his disquietude he had formed an obscure plan of charity. Yet at the same time he understood that such an undertaking was none of his business; he knew nothing of Teiji Yamamoto. One did not change the world with a few words.

"What did he say?" asked Teiji Yamamoto. The tremble was still apparent.

"Before he died, he spoke your name."

"Anything more?"

"He said you would be an artist."

"Yes, he did? What else?"

"This was wartime."

"I see."

"He spoke through another soldier," Kleinman said, anticipating a question he had not thought of until that moment. "They had both been hit. When your father died, your name was on his lips. He was a courageous man." Kleinman paused. "He was a fine artist," he said. "And he gave me the letter, which I was attempting to bring to your mother."

Teiji Yamamoto, sipping his tea, appeared to be thinking. "Then you cannot tell me anything more?"

"I'm afraid I cannot." Kleinman moved his tea aside. "But I have this for you," he said. From the stone floor he lifted the burlap packet and loosened the drawn mouth. Teiji Yamamoto watched him, his eyes visibly following the movements of Kleinman's hands. Kleinman opened the sack, lifted out the stiff palette, which had the weight and heft of a hardbound book, its stack of pages still neatly bound in thick, grayed twine. He set it on the wooden table, loosened the ties, lifted the first translucent sheet from the pile, and held it to the light. He had no idea what it said. There must have been fifty others, and all he had seen of them, he realized now, was the letter that had hung above his mantel for decades and the two odd pages of musings, which had been displayed obscurely in the stairwell in the house in Squirrel Hill. He marveled at his own incuriosity. After the framer had left, thirty years ago, he had never opened the sack again, had merely set it downstairs on a high shelf next to his old army duffel and a sextet of poorly engraved beer steins given to him by Mayor Barr of Pittsburgh before an election. But holding the rice paper now, he saw immediately that the surface had been cleaned—by the framer, he realized with a sudden touch of satisfaction—and he noticed that between the pages the man had also set layers of protective backing. He set down the first sheet in front of Teiji Yamamoto, whose eyes dropped to the crowded lines of script. His hands were trembling like a drunkard's.

"Here," Kleinman said. "Why don't I hold your tea?"

"Yes, yes, of course."

Kleinman reached across quickly and lifted the cup himself, fearing that if Teiji Yamamoto touched it, it would capsize. "I'll leave you here with these, then. I have a plane out of Tokyo this evening."

"Yes."

He watched as Teiji Yamamoto scanned the pages. "I don't know what they say," Kleinman said. He was looking for some clue in the other man's face, but Teiji Yamamoto was moving too rapidly through the stack, reading for a moment from one sheet, lifting the next, spreading them out before him like a set of ancient maps.

"Perhaps they will be important to you," Kleinman said. "I hope they are."

"Yes, yes."

Kleinman stood. Teiji Yamamoto paused for the first time to look up at him, and Kleinman saw that tears were streaking his cheeks; but at the same time his mouth, held tightly closed, was turned up at the corners, and the small choked wheezes he made sounded to Kleinman something like laughter. He reached up and

gripped Kleinman's forearm. With his other hand he was still trac-
ing the lines of script before him. Kleinman patted the fingers. At
Ginger's funeral, Hannah had wept the same way, holding Kleinman's arm, smiling tentatively beneath her tears whenever he
looked down at her beside him, as though there was something
even greater now between the two of them than had been there
before—as though even then could be heard some overtone
of joy.

Kleinman left the teahouse, but it was not until he was seated
again in the car that he let loose and wept. His guide glanced
quickly across at him, then turned back and stared straight ahead
at the driver; but this did not reduce Kleinman's enjoyment of the
sobbing. In the chill wind from the open window, the activity felt
something like exercise. He bellowed and shook, then thrust his
head out the window to clear it. Finally, he said, "It's okay, sweetheart. We're all going to be fine."

For the return trip in the funicular, she sat next to him and insisted on naming all the mountains as they descended in the cool
late-morning air toward Gora. "Mount Kami," she said, pointing
her finger through the car's curved front windows as they moved
down the steep hillside amid the fluttering gold and auburn leaves.
"Mount Myojyogatake," she added, nodding vigorously as though
he had asked her some question about the densely forested peaks
beyond them.

"Don't worry," Kleinman said. "I'm not going to cry anymore."

"No, no."

"You don't do that here, I know. We don't either, in America.
Not usually, at least. Powerful emotions came over me. It was a

very moving situation. I'm fine now, though. You don't have to worry." For some reason he found himself turning to her and popping his lips, the way Jimmy had while changing Asher. Then he smiled. "All done," he said.

"Ah, yes, yes. Sometimes cry here, too. Ah, look, we are here now at Gora. We take train to Odawara, then Tokyo. Yes?"

"No car, huh? Your driver didn't like us hopping out in the middle of the road, I guess."

"No, no, we take train because it is very pretty. Autumn leaves."

From Odawara they caught the high-speed line back toward Tokyo. The car was crowded, and Kleinman found himself sitting several rows in front of her, sipping from a can of cold Japanese beer and watching the country disappear behind them as he considered what he had done. Given more time, he might have answered Teiji Yamamoto differently about what had occurred so long ago; but the question had surprised him. That was how ignorant he still was of the human being; he thought of Jimmy, of his sullenness, his nervous meticulousness with a punch line. What might his children ask about him? Or he, if he could, about his own father? Loss, in time, became a physical sensation; and from there, over more time, a puzzle—fading, at last, until it could no longer be held. The train streaked north. Alongside the track, steep hills of an aqueous green hue climbed to the west, fields of tea or perhaps winter wheat that rose to tiny towns peeking like castle mounts through the thick covering of pines. Greenery, water, settlement, the enduring journey of children: the world was the same in every corner of its reach.

~~~~~~~~~~~~~~~~~~~~~~~~~~~~~

Kleinman was sitting in Asher's room when the door opened. It was past midnight. In the dim light he watched Claudine move next to the crib, lean down, look in, look back up. "Jesus!" she said.

"Shhh," he whispered. "It's just me, Grandpa Augie."

"You scared me! What are you doing in here?"

"Watching your boy."

"You are?"

"Yes."

"How long have you been doing that?"

"All night. I just want to make sure his noggin is all right."

"You're so sweet," she said.

"Don't tell anyone."

She sat down on the stool in the corner, next to where he was leaning back in the rocker. He and Ginger used to sit like this after Harry was born. "Well," she said. "It's been really nice having you."

"And for me a pleasure too."

"You know, you could have this pleasure all the time."

"Yes, I know."

"Why don't you move closer?"

"I don't think I want to."

"I don't see why you don't jump at the idea," she said. "I can see you're lonely. Anybody can see that. You could spend your time with us, with your grandson."

"It's not that. That, I would love."

"What is it then?"

"It's that moving back home, coming back to New York, leaving what I have in Boston. I would only be coming back—never mind."

She cleared her throat. "I think I know what you're going to say."

Asher stirred on the mattress. Kleinman said, "I'd only be coming back to die."

He felt something on his shoulder—her hand.

"And I don't want to," he said. "Not yet. That's just me. Why shouldn't I? I've got my children, but they all have their own lives. Me? I've got nothing left to live for. It's all gone. And the end is getting nearer. I know that. Don't think I can't feel it. But I don't give up. That's just Augie Kleinman. I always thought I had a secret, that when the end came I would be ready for it—that the grave would be a relief. But it turns out it's not that way."

"You're not ready for it."

"Not in the least. Men like me—we get wrestled into the coffin. That, I'll tell you. Look—let's not talk about it anymore."

"Well in that case, maybe you can just visit more often."

"That, I plan to."

"It was lovely having you."

"And likewise. You made a delicious dinner tonight."

She was silent. Asher stirred in the crib, raised his leg in a dream, and then dropped it. Finally, Claudine said, "You must have been hungry."

"I was."

"It's a long fast."

"That it is."

"Tell me," she said. "You say you're not devout, but you fast all day."

"It's not a question of religion. It's a question of discipline and respect. Respect for my father. My stepfather, that is. The man who raised me and gave my mother such happiness. He would have wanted me to."

She was silent again. Hank Kleinman used to wear a prayer shawl in the house. His brother, Izzy, still wore one, Kleinman supposed, though he hadn't seen him in twenty years. He was living in Arizona, married to a woman who didn't like him to see his family. The world turns.

"By the way," Claudine said. "I suppose it was Asher eating the asparagus."

"Pardon?"

"You left the bowl here." In the dim light, she pointed to the cabinet.

"Ah," said Kleinman. "I see I did."

"It's all right," she said. "*Pikuakh nefesh.*"

"Amen."

"And I had some cottage cheese myself."

"You did?"

"Don't tell your son."

"Never," Kleinman said. He laughed, rocking back in the dark.

This girl, she was something—Jimmy was going to be all right, after all.

~~~~~~~~~~~~~~~~~~~~~~~~~~~~~~~~~~

What to do with his riches? He'd spoken to a high-priced estate planner on Boylston Street, who'd encouraged him in the direction of life insurance—ungodly premiums now, but the estate transferred upon his passing without any taxes at all—a feat of legerdemain unequaled in his experience with Internal Revenue. The man wore pomade in his hair. Kleinman distrusted him, distrusted the scheme, distrusted the system of inherited wealth in its entirety. But nonetheless he needed to decide how to dispense with his money. In truth, he didn't mind giving his share to the government, but he didn't want them using it on bombs. When he explained this to the estate planner, the man's face showed a trismic flinch, as though an electric current had been suddenly emitted from the walnut desk. And there were his charities to take care of as well. Kleinman didn't mind giving a good bit to his children, of course; but to give them too much, he knew, was an invitation to ruin. He'd sipped enough mimosas with Carnegies in Christmas jackets.

Harry would put the money in the bank, give some of it away to liberal charities, maybe buy a beachfront place on the Gulf coast of Texas or even in the Yucatán; Hannah would put it in her checking account, no doubt, where it would sit for years, would touch it only to purchase obscure volumes of French poetry while the bankers skimmed the earnings—he'd have to remember to find her a good financial planner. But what would Jimmy do with it? He didn't know. Quit his job? That's what worried him, that Jimmy would somehow see it as his due, its long-delayed arrival the only hindrance in his plans. But Claudine seemed sensible. Perhaps not as frugal as he liked, but smart enough to be aware of the damage riches could do. As he waited for his plane at La Guardia, he considered his options.

In December of 1970, at Ginger's suggestion, he invited his mother and Hank Kleinman along for a weekend, expenses paid, in Miami Beach, where he was traveling for a convention of East Coast brewers and distillers. By then, the two of them were in their seventies and Kleinman's relations with them had grown infrequent. He flew to New York to pick them up—again at Ginger's suggestion—then took a cab from La Guardia to the Jamaica station of the Long Island Rail Road so that he could get on a train, because that's how he wanted to arrive again in Wavecrest. He hadn't been home in almost twenty years. When he came out of the station, he had to look at a map to confirm he'd not gotten off at the wrong stop. He recognized almost nothing. He didn't go directly to the flat, but in the confounding remains of his old neighborhood found himself wandering west along the water, his small bag over his shoulder. The boardwalk was still there, but the old hotels—where the better families, the families of grocers and schoolteachers and policemen, had stayed on their trips fleeing the Manhattan summer—had been converted into what looked like boardinghouses, or perhaps nursing homes, and all the old businesses had closed. Not just closed—they'd been razed. There were unrecognizable buildings everywhere, and in some places mere holes in the ground, sliced by the rain-gutted tracks of bulldozers. The tobacconist's, the newsstand with its Yiddish papers, Mr. Kemmerer's violin and viola shop, the barber with the wooden ice-cream cart he pedaled on weekend afternoons—all had been swallowed by the earth. He wasn't even sure where he was. The blocks west of Beach 50th had become a ghetto, and the rows of bungalows he remembered from his childhood had been leveled for a set of brick public housing projects that ran one after the other along the littered coast toward Hammels. He looked up at the rows of square metal tenement windows facing bleakly out onto the water. But when he turned to the south all he saw was the ocean again, tiled with blown whitecaps, and it could easily have been a Sunday afternoon in 1941: there was Ginger on a blanket in the sand with two of her prettiest sisters, and up the boardwalk, leaning against a bench, with Hank Kleinman beside her, was his mother in her blue woolen coat. The waves showed their winter edge of slate.

He turned and walked home toward Beach 28th. There was enough in the world to feel sorry for without mourning the change of one small neighborhood. People came and went; buildings fell and rose. Here was just the newest wave in the world's endless tide of aspirants. Sorrow was irrelevant, at least for a thing like this. But he was pleased to discover nonetheless that his own building hadn't changed at all, still showed the same weathered triangle of unfaded mustard paint in the shadow of the roof peak and the blistered black window trim that was peeling in long streaks like zebra hide to the white primer beneath. Standing on the ledges were some dead plants in pots. On the terrazzo stairs of the entranceway the cold smell of salty broth made him feel suddenly like a child again, late for Shabbes dinner. When his mother answered the door, he saw that something was terribly wrong.

"Oh, Augie," she said.

"What is it, Ma?"

"I've been like this for weeks."

August took her hand. She was swollen as a tick. Her neck was pressed into a fiery red band by the collar of her blouse, her arms were straining against her bunched-up sleeves, and her legs bulged below her hemline as though half her torso had slid down into her stockings. She had slit her shoes to accommodate her feet. "My God," Kleinman said. "Why didn't you tell anybody?"

"We didn't want to worry you."

"Have you seen the doctor?"

"What can the doctor do?"

Hank Kleinman, thin as a lamppost, shuffled out of the back room then in his tallith to hug him, smelling of cherry-tinged cigar smoke, and Kleinman could feel him weeping as they embraced. He was mumbling the Hebrew prayers. "Your mother," he said. "Something's wrong."

"I can see that."

"I think maybe a spider bite," said Hank Kleinman. "The block is filthy now. They're in the house."

"Oh, Augie, I don't know if we can go to Miami. Maybe Hank can go without me."

"Don't be ridiculous, Mom. Nobody's going to Miami."

He wished they had told him sooner, but when he considered the possibilities, he was grateful for how it had turned out. They had let him come up to fetch them, at least—that meant something. Their relations by then had been strained for years, not by bitterness or acrimony but merely by the tiny, uncrossable divide of religion. His heart ached at this sometimes, but for him there was no going back and for Hank Kleinman no going forward. August canceled his reservations for Florida and got on the phone to a man he knew at Pitt, who called them back in an hour with an appointment at the private office of a cardiologist on faculty at NYU. He spent the next six days in Wavecrest, shuttling his mother in taxicabs back and forth from Manhattan. It wasn't a spider bite; it was heart failure. But she was given a set of pills and, on the new regimen, grew rapidly better. Her skin lost its tensioned sheen; the wrinkles on her fingers reemerged, her feet slipped back into her shoes.

This visit was when Kleinman first understood that his mother, somehow, had been left behind by the world. She'd come to America from a prosperous but bitter household, had left behind in Hamburg a dour mansion of statuary, French cooking, and string quartets to come ashore as a subject in a plain but truthful second kingdom. How could she know then that its borders would grow close, tightened and tightened by the godly arcana of her new husband's piety? August felt gratitude and affection for Hank Kleinman, but now that the neighborhood was no longer Jewish, it was also clear that their lives had been drawn like nooses around them. Hank Kleinman was a convivial man but would not, somehow, cross a border. Before August's visit, his mother probably hadn't been to Manhattan in a decade. And when the Jewish businesses closed, they simply did without. They probably didn't even know a doctor.

And all this at the same time that his own life was expanding outward like a whirligig. From a brazen young salesman with a knuckleheaded idea, he had grown into a force and fixture in Pittsburgh commerce—he went to parties now with Mayor Barr and Mayor Flaherty; he could pick up the phone in the morning and be sitting that afternoon in the owner's box at the new Three Rivers Stadium, watching the surging Pirates; when he threw a party, he hired Carnegie-Mellon students to park the cars. Borders for him had become memories only. Nothing more. He felt unencumbered. Light in the world.

Nonetheless, when he returned home from New York he was badly shaken. He had never in all his days been depressed—it was neither a term nor a feeling he understood—but over the following months in Pittsburgh, months in which he telephoned Wavecrest every evening, he felt blackened by memory, darkly perturbed every moment by the suggestion of loss. His childhood neighborhood. His mother. He even returned in his mind to the house on Herrengraben, the specter of it fallen into the hands of his father's assassins. He had always looked forward in his life, peered ahead around every corner: this was how he had gotten where he was. But then one afternoon on the brewery's loading dock, waiting for a late truckful of Washington State hops, he found himself in tears. Inexplicable, really; except that he knew he was weeping—fifteen years too early, as it turned out, thanks to the cardiologist—for the death of his mother.

Christoph Cerny, on the dock next to him, said, "What is this, my friend?"

"My mother, that's all."

"I am sorry. I did not know."

"She's ill. She looked terrible when I saw her. I hadn't seen her in so long, I hadn't known anything was wrong."

Kleinman told him the story, and Christoph Cerny gave him some good, sound advice. "Don't visit over the religious holiday," he said immediately, cupping his elephantine hands over Kleinman's. "Simple. You visit on birthday. You make them celebrate the American holiday—Thanksgiving. No religion. You will all be better for it. Yes?"

November 2, 1996
San Antonio, Texas

Dear Mr. Kleinman,

I received the news of your wife's passing this week and am writing to express my deepest sympathy. My husband never forgot you and sometimes spoke of what you said. I know he would have wanted to express these con-dolences himself.

May you find courage in these trying days.

Most sincerely yours,

—Lady Bird Johnson

In the morning, Kleinman was already packed, was closing the locks on his valise, when Jimmy entered and sat down on the bed. "Hey, Pop, let me help with those buckles."

"And then what? I call a locksmith on the other end?"

Jimmy was quiet. He rose from the bed and looked incuriously at his father.

"Well," Kleinman finally offered, fiddling with the tiny keys. "I have two things wrong with me now. Did I tell you?" He set the valise on its side and went to retrieve his jacket from the closet. His plane was leaving in two hours. "Now *that's* something," he said. "When I had the heart problems, I thought it was the worst thing that could ever happen. But now it's something else."

"What is it, Pop?"

Kleinman removed the sheet of paper from his wallet and un-folded it. On it was written: *myelodysplastic syndrome.*

"What's that?"

"Frankly, I don't know. Dr. Wolff sent me to a blood man, Dr. Stern. Stern and Wolff," he said, folding the jacket inside-out for the car ride. "Perhaps not a good sign. Dr. Stern told me it could be something serious at any time, though for the time being, it is not serious. I have a few years at least. That's what he told me, if you can believe it. The rest I didn't want to know. Could at any time be serious, but for the time being it is not serious. What do you think of that diagnosis? I asked Dr. Stern how such a state of affairs was any different from simply being alive. He laughed."

"Is it cancer, Pop?"

"No. I don't think so."

Jimmy stood and went to the window. Looking out, he said, "So, are you really leaving us?"

"Well—" Kleinman began. Then he realized he had misunderstood. "I'll come back," he answered. "Anytime you want. But I already have my tickets."

A t the Au Bon Pain near Harvard Square, he met Isabela within a couple of hours of his return to Boston. Aida was with her, only recently bold enough to even stand next to him. She slouched a few feet from the table and stared silently while he asked her his questions about kindergarten. She looked like a girl watching a tiger at the zoo. Isabela tugged at her long black hair with a plastic comb and urged her in Spanish to answer, but she wouldn't. Kleinman didn't mind. The plaza was filled with families—young mothers and fathers wrangling their children, sitting them in high chairs, strapping them into strollers, buttoning them into coats. On the great sea of life these people were still on the outward journey; he, on the other hand, was on his way back. Tiny perturbations did not unsettle him. The morning was filled with the chill and gusts of gathering winter.

"I'll be going away for a few days," he said to Isabela.

"When?" she asked.

"Day after tomorrow." He knew she would not ask him where. It was not lack of interest but a conviction about her own fragile station. He wondered how a woman could make it in this country alone and still maintain such deference. She excited in him his old protectiveness. "I'm going to Japan," he said.

"Are you never coming back?" Aida blurted.

"Of course I am, sweetheart," he said, and she allowed him to pat her hair. How that told him what he'd never known! Now she was making a pouting face at him, a gesture of brazen intimacy. He made one back. She laughed, a first for her. Earlier that morning he had bought a sequined barrette in a dime store at the corner, and now he thanked the Lord for his foresight and produced it for her from the pocket of his coat. He felt like a great lover, his timing unmatchable. Or perhaps he was only a great salesman. "And here's something for you, too," he said to Isabela.

He never liked this moment, because it made her a supplicant. But she was a practical woman with difficulties greater than his own, and this always redeemed her, gave her strength despite the flush of embarrassment on her olive cheeks. She slid the envelope into her purse without looking at it. "Oh no," she said, as she always did.

"Oh yes," Kleinman answered. "You know I don't need it."

By the time she opened it, he would be over the Pacific Ocean. Of course, they would question her at the bank. But who cared? There was plenty more. They'd probably even call his brokers at Mellon for verification. This would be a humiliation, but in her features there was the grace, again, that all could see, even a teller at a bank.

～～～～～～～～～～～～～～～～

The flight back from Tokyo was difficult. He felt vertiginous in the airport and at one point was obliged to hold on to a column while the sea of suits tilted around him. In his carry-on he had a bottle of Dramamine, but he made his way to the United lounge instead to wait out the attack. This had happened to him once before, on a flight from Boston to New York that he'd boarded with the flu. That's when he'd been prescribed the Dramamine. But he didn't want to take it. Doctors always wanted to give you things: a little of this, a little of that. Before long it was one medicine against another. The whole approach negated the effects of self-control. In the United lounge, he concentrated on the horizon out the window but was afraid to rise from his seat. The Japanese businessmen around him drank sake, talked on portable phones, played with miniature electronic games that beeped and gave off tinny chimes and music in their hands. The vertigo appeared whenever he moved his head, so he sat perfectly still. After a while he gave in, found the bottle of Dramamine, and inquired of the agent for a glass of water. When she asked if she should order a wheelchair, he said, without moving his head, "Only if you need one."

In Japan, people didn't understand his humor.

In first class he didn't see any other Caucasians. He'd made it to his seat, the one farthest back in the compartment, by holding the rope at the gate, then the rail on the gangway, then the wall of the plane, then the headrests. A delay was announced, and the stewardess walked around with a tray of champagne. The delay was all right with Kleinman, but the champagne as a tactic seemed coarse. The Japanese men seemed juvenile to him as well; they wore thousand-dollar suits but played electronic games and drank while the plane was still waiting to leave the ground. These were the men in the jungle. Next to him a young man was reading a paperback book that appeared to be a bodice-ripper. The Japanese characters looked comical below the picture of a thinly clad young woman. Kleinman took a sip of champagne, handed back the glass, and lowered his seat. The rest of the bulbs were in his carry-on, and for some reason he took them out and lifted the velvet sack up against his chest.

He might have slept. Something demanded his attention. The man next to him was snoring now, the paperback over his face. The scene outside the window was still Tokyo, baggage trucks moving alongside the runway. The stewardess smiled at him. This was no small delay. Ginger was going to be upset, but that was how it always was. In this instance there was nothing he could do. Inside the fuselage came the sickening smell of jet fuel; then the lights blinked and the air system came on above them. The Dramamine was making him drowsy. He smiled and closed his eyes. *We're in no hurry.* Not now, at least. He could feel sleep like a blanket. The fans had blown away the fuel smell and the air was chilly now. *Wake me up, my love. It's cold in here.*

The moisture was cool on his face suddenly, and the rush of water in earnest: he was inside the lip of the cavern. He stood flattened against the wall, straining to see into the dark. Then, underneath the roar of the waterfall, he heard the boar. It was off to his left and some distance away, perhaps along the facing wall. He stood unmoving, his Garand pointed low. The sound came no closer: there might be a lake between them. He lowered himself to a squat. He touched the flashlight switch, his hand shaking. The snorts were confusing, mixed with the waterfall. He heard them low and to his left, nine o'clock and at the level of the floor. *I love you Ginger, I am thinking of you always.* One mistake here and he was dead. He flipped the flashlight switch on and off.

The soldier was on his stomach, the ammo belt crossed behind him. He knew he had three more steps, and in his mind he fixed the position of the body so that he could move in the dark: behind him was a pillar of rock, high as a refrigerator. That's where he would go. Another step. Recheck the safety. Two feet away now. There could be soldiers in other rooms. When he sensed he was next to the pillar, he unscabbarded the bayonet and listened for other sounds in the cave. Then a prayer. All that came to him was the Kaddish: *Yit-ga-dal v'yit-ka-dash*—halfway through, the words failed him. Ginger. Della again, asleep in her bed. He felt for the pillar and stepped behind it. Then he hid all but a sliver of the flashlight lens in his fingers; either he would die in a storm of bul-

lets or he would be saved. He flipped it on and off. Below him on
the rock floor the soldier lay snoring, his belt crossed on his back
at the level of the heart. Then suddenly the snoring stopped.

A match.

Kleinman pulled himself in to the rear of the pillar. He was hiding behind a rock now. Hiding behind a rock! Like a children's
game! He made himself thin behind it, standing mortally frightened while from around the other side he heard the Jap rise
quickly to his feet. The release of a safety. Steps. Then suddenly
the walls of the cavern were bright, flickering with candlelight.
Then brighter and steady: a lamp. A shadow moved onto the single wall that Kleinman could see. Behind the rock, he pulled back
again, too terrified to move; the shadow disappeared beyond the
edge of his vision. The footsteps continued, so soft beneath the
sound of the waterfall that Kleinman's ears were going to come off
his head! Then, suddenly, a voice in Japanese—in a moment the
enemy would come streaming in. *I love you Ginger. I am thinking of
you—please think of me at this moment!* The soldier kept talking. He
was going on at length. Abruptly, Kleinman realized there were
English words mixed in. "See GI Joe! See GI Joe!" Then more
Japanese. Then, "See GI Joe!" The soldier was talking to him!
Maybe the man was alone! At that moment he moved into Kleinman's view again, holding his rifle at his side and gesturing at the
wall with a lantern. There must be more soldiers around! Suddenly
Kleinman saw that he was pointing to a map on the wall. The soldier swung the lantern to illuminate it, then set it down and picked
up something else—a book. He was pointing with it and beckon-
ing. Then he set down his rifle and pointed at the wall with both

hands. He set down his rifle! What in hell was happening? He was trying to bluff him out of hiding! That's what was happening! But then he picked up the lantern again, shone it on the far wall, and began gesturing there with the book. Now Kleinman saw that there were also other pillars over there! Several of them—this was what had confused the enemy! This was what was going to save him! The Jap turned the book toward the tunnel where Kleinman had come in. But the rifle was still on the ground! This was a decoy! Could he be alone? No, the talking was a signal to his comrades! There could be more rooms behind the other pillars! The book was a trick! So was the gun! He could shoot now. But the rifle report would give him away. He lifted the bayonet. Then the Jap turned from the entrance, moved across the room, and was lost. "See GI Joe!" Then more Japanese. The voice seemed to be coming from the high roof. Kleinman tried to trace the route of the approaching footsteps. They were closing on him steadily. The Jap had seen his footprints! That's what it was! Kleinman gripped the Garand with two hands, raised the bayonet, and crouched. The lantern was no longer lighting his view. Either the Jap would appear to his right, where he would have a glimpse of his back, or he would come up on the left and that would be the end for Kleinman, no sound (did death come too fast for that?); two Jap slugs in the head; the Shema failed him; his thoughts went out instead to Ginger again, asleep—*I adore you*—and to his brother, Izzy, on the beach at Rockaway, and then around the far side of the pillar came a click as soft as a chewed cracker and the Jap was there to the right without his rifle, holding out the book and looking the wrong way, dark clips crossed over his back at the level of the heart, which Kleinman, exploding forward, struck through with the bayonet like a tiger.

The man staggered, then dropped. Kleinman pulled back the blade and struck again, pinning the chest to the floor. Then he yanked it free and scrambled back behind the pillar. The body seized, slapping against the rock. Then it was still. Kleinman crouched in his hiding place. The lantern had fallen over, and the room was dark again. He heard nothing but the roar of the waterfall. After a time, he reached out with the bayonet and felt for the body. Then, from behind the pillar, he shone his own flashlight quickly around the cavern: no other soldiers. He switched it off again and waited. Finally, he turned it on and crept out into the open. The soldier lay in a lake of blood. The room was no more than a dozen feet long; he checked behind all the pillars, but the only entrance was the one he had used. Along the far side was the map sketched upon the flattest face of the rock. He turned the flashlight on it. It had been drawn with colors—bright even in the weak light: dark blues and greens, bits of gold. He tried to commit its essentials to memory, then suddenly realized it was not a map at all but a painting of a mountain—it looked like Mount Fuji—drawn upside down; trees were bundled in thickly along the foreground. In the corner ran a stream that had been incorporated into the vista, plummeting from the ceiling and dropping away through a hole in the limestone. This was the waterfall he had heard. He shone the light around the circumference, then up into the narrow passage where he had entered. There were no signs of anyone else. The man had been alone. Through the stream hole came a wash of cool air. On the floor were some ration tins, candles, an ammunition box, and the rifle. Kleinman emptied it. The soldier's arm rested near the book, and when Kleinman opened it, he saw it contained plates of Oriental paintings, now darkened with blood. On a ledge he found a small pile of other books, which he quickly examined: one seemed to be an operations manual, which his C.O. would want, and one was a journal, sheaves of rice paper tied in a packet, filled with neat Japanese characters. He shoved it into his belt. The others seemed to be more volumes of paintings. He took the dog tags and folded them into the operations manual, then slid both into his pocket. The sound in the cave now was the chattering of his own teeth. He felt the neck for a pulse, then turned, passed quickly through the cavern, and squeezed himself back into the tunnel.

Something pushed down on his shoulder. The stewardess said, "Sir, you'll need to put your seat in the upright position for take-off."

"I can do what I want."

"Captain Bradford is unable to move until you do."

"There's nobody behind me. I'll keep my chair as I please."

"Come on, old geezer!" someone shouted.

"I like that!" Kleinman shouted back. "Geezer yourself!"

"Sir, you'll need to move your seat back up. Here—"

"All right. I'm moving."

Someone clapped. As soon as the chair was upright, the plane began to roll, a big, slow turn onto the runway. Outside, the world warped by jet fumes.

Now they were moving on the tarmac. He said the Kaddish. Once again it failed him. He lifted the sack of bulbs to his face and smelled it: earth, vinegar-sweetness. He was lifting Asher: I will protect you all the days of my life. He was lifting the baby Teiji to dip him in the lake. He was lifting Jimmy, soaked in blood. He was lifting Ginger. He let his mouth touch the cloth. Kiss the Torah: he hadn't done that in fifty years. Too sure of his own thinking. Who did you apologize to for that? The velvet was cool on his lips. Next to him, the Japanese man glanced over, glanced away. They were at speed now. He lowered his chair back again. The stewardess looked up and shook her finger at him. Breathe deep. Asher, the sweet smell of his head. The plane roared and tilted; in his chest the lightness of escape, then lift.

ABOUT THE AUTHOR

ETHAN CANIN is the author of *Emperor of the Air, The Palace Thief,* and *For Kings and Planets.* He is on the faculty of the University of Iowa Writers' Workshop, and is also a physician. He lives in California and Iowa.

ABOUT THE TYPE

This book was set in Weiss, a typeface designed by a German artist, Emil Rudolf Weiss (1875–1942). The designs of the roman and italic fonts were completed in 1928 and 1931 respectively. The Weiss types are rich, well-balanced, and even in color, and they reflect the subtle skill of a fine calligrapher.